George Weddell

Arcana Fairfaxiana Manuscripta

A manuscript volume of apothecaries' lore and housewifery nearly three centuries

old, used, and partly written by the Fairfax family

George Weddell

Arcana Fairfaxiana Manuscripta
A manuscript volume of apothecaries' lore and housewifery nearly three centuries old, used, and partly written by the Fairfax family

ISBN/EAN: 9783337596606

Printed in Europe, USA, Canada, Australia, Japan

Cover: Foto ©Andreas Hilbeck / pixelio.de

More available books at **www.hansebooks.com**

Arcana Fairfaxiana

Manuscripta.

A manuscript volume of Apothecaries' Lore and
Housewifery nearly three centuries old,
used, and partly written by the
Fairfax Family.

———

Reproduced in fac-simile of the handwritings.

———

An Introduction by
George Weddell.

———

Newcastle-on-Tyne:
Mawson, Swan, & Morgan.
—
mdcccxc.

Acknowledgments.

To Markham's "Life of Lord Fairfax," and to the "Fairfax Correspondence," I am indebted for most of my information regarding that eminent family. My thanks are due to gentlemen of the British Museum, who, beyond the courtesy always to be met with in that National Institution, freely gave me during my searches the benefit of their own reading and experience.

To the Reader.

References are made in the Introduction to the paging at the *foot* of the Manuscript, not to the original numbers at the head, which are irregular. From this irregular paging it will be gathered that there were numerous blank pages between various sections of the book, which of course have not been inserted in the reproduction. Should any reader find much difficulty in deciphering a particular portion which may be interesting to him, I shall be pleased to send a transcription; and should there be a sufficiently expressed desire for a type edition of the book, nothing need stand in the way. There will, however, be no reprint of the fac-simile.

G. W.

Table of Contents.

The Story of the Book.

THOSE who are interested in this book will probably desire to learn something of its history, and of the people who have at various times possessed it. The most interesting way to give this information will perhaps be to describe how I found the book, and to follow the various steps by which I traced its origin, as far as that is known.

About seven years ago, during the re-arrangement for business purposes of some rooms at 135, Pilgrim Street, Newcastle-on-Tyne, which for a hundred years have been occupied by the firm of Gilpin & Co., Chemists, in which I am associated, I observed in a box of lumber a leather-bound volume, which on examination I found to be in manuscript. Having rescued it from destruction, I carefully examined all other consignments for the dustbin, and found several books of a certain interest, but none of the same value and charm as the first, which is herein reproduced in fac-simile.

From time to time I examined the book, contenting myself at first with such portions as were most plainly written, until the interest which I found in the quaint language and curious remedies led me to study it more minutely and to search for internal evidence of its age and writers.

This was of a very fragmentary nature. The reference on page 30 to "An electuary yᵗ Quene Mary was wont to take for yᵉ passion of yᵉ hart," only hinted that this portion of the book was written after her time—an indefinite period. "Quene Elizabeth" also, when page 63 was written, might have been either in the present or the past. The book of "Rodolphus Goclerius, professor of Phisicke in Wittenburghe," which was published in 1608 and mentioned on page 61, might have been many years old before the gruesome recipe was copied.

Coming to a succeeding portion of the book, however, there appeared to be a lively sympathy between the writer and the names mentioned. "My Lady Fairfax, of Steeton, Feb. 25th, 1632," (page 135), seemed a person of present interest, and the other names of Cholmeley, Sheffield, Selby, Widdrington, and others were too thickly strewn to be those of a past generation. Selecting the historic family of Fairfax for my first line of research, and the "Life of Lord Fairfax," by Mr. Clements Markham, as my first book, I learned that the parliamentary general of that name in the time of Charles I. was intimately related to most of the persons mentioned in that part of the manuscript. Ell. Fairfax, Lady Selby, Lady Widdrington, and Mrs. Dorothy Hutton were his sisters, Lady Constable was his aunt, and Lady Bellasis his great-aunt. Sir Ferd. Fairfax was his father, Sheffield was his mother's maiden name, and others mentioned in the book were his cousins or kinsfolk.

This suggested to me that the Fairfax family might have been the original owners of the book, but the initials M. C. stamped in gold on the binding dispelled for a time this idea. In the handwriting of that portion there appears on page 132 a note, " See my brother Hen. Cholmeley's book." Was it a Cholmeley, then, who had entered the recipes, and signed them so frequently with the initials H. C.? From what I could learn of that family there were about the middle of the 17th century two brothers, Sir Hugh and Sir Henry, and from the note just mentioned it seemed possible that the former had written it. On tracing his handwriting in the British Museum, however, I found it entirely unlike my manuscript. By investigating the relationship between the Fairfaxes and the Cholmeleys, I found that the Hon. and Rev. Henry Fairfax, uncle to the great parliamentary general, had married Mary, daughter of Sir Henry Cholmeley, of Whitby. This Sir Henry Cholmeley was the grandfather of the Hugh and Henry mentioned above and the father of another Henry and numerous children besides Mary. It appeared quite possible, therefore, that the initals M. C. on the cover referred to Mary, and that she had brought the book to her husband's house on her marriage. It seemed also possible that she herself was the writer of that portion where " My brother Hen. Cholmeley " was mentioned. In the Bodleian Library, however, I found several female handwritings of the period, and of the family, so unlike it, that I renounced the latter idea. It had also occurred to me that her husband might naturally call Henry Cholmeley by the affectionate title of brother. I then sought for the writing of Henry Fairfax, and on a subsequent visit to the British Museum, discovered a specimen of it in the exact hand of my book. As if with the object of assisting me, the piece consisted of " A note of suche nephewes and neeces as are or were allyed to us H. and M. F. when Feb. 10th 1635 " (add MSS. 11,335, fol. 48). This list of nephews and nieces, to the modest number of 137, included many of the names mentioned in my book, which I had not previously been able to link with the Fairfaxes. Besides other specimens of Henry's writing, I also found several letters in Mary's own hand, two of which have been published in the "Fairfax Correspondence" (vol. 1, fol. 62, 64). Her writing I recognised as one which occurs in several parts of this book, so I had thus the pleasure of verifying two at least of the actual writers. Other members of the family had also added small portions,— Sir Ferdinando Fairfax, Sir Henry Cholmeley already referred to, and Henry Fairfax's son Brian. The writing of the latter is not so certain as the others, being a current hand of the period, written somewhat carelessly; and although much of Brian's work in the British Museum clearly resembles that which I ascribe to him in the "Arcana," yet, on occasion, he wrote a large, flowing "magnificent" hand, probably assumed for the purpose of diplomatic effect.

It now occurred to me to enquire how Mary Cholmeley's initials came to be stamped upon the cover of the book. That such a volume, essentially belonging to the head of a household, should have been made expressly for an unmarried lady, seemed highly unlikely; and had it been presented to her on her marriage in 1626, it would have borne the initials M. F. instead of M. C. Another possibility remained, namely, that her mother's name also might have been Mary, and that the book had been hers. A subsequent search revealed the fact that her mother was Margaret, a daughter of Sir William Babthorpe, and the initials M. C. were, therefore, appropriate to her also. Another piece of circumstantial evidence appeared on the last page of the book in the form of " A note of Mistress Barbara; her lessons on ye Virginalle," written in one of the early hands. Now Mary was, I think, the seventh child and fifth daughter of her parents, her eldest sister being named Barbara. Mary was born in 1593, Barbara certainly not later than 1584, as about 1634 she had at least six married children, a circumstance which rarely happens to a lady before the age of fifty. Some time, therefore, about 1600, this Barbara was a young lady of the period, probably learning to play on the virginal the music of the eminent composer William Bird, Organist to Queen Elizabeth, and of the more recent Dr. Bull, who was then at the height of his fame. The latter took his degree of Mus. Doc. in 1592, and I think that, while the " Note of Mistress Barbara " could not possibly have been writen earlier than that time, it was probably written before 1610. If this were the same Barbara,—which the small initials B. C. on that page almost prove, it must have been much nearer the earlier date.

Whether the book actually belonged to Mary Cholmeley or to her mother is not absolutely certain ; but

I think it undoubtedly belonged to one of them. I suggest, however, from the evidence shown, that it was made for the use of the latter, Margaret Cholmeley, wife of Sir Henry Cholmeley, and that the writings numbered I. to IV. in the succeeding notes were executed during the " Cholmeley period," that is at various reasonable dates previous to 1626. In that year Mary, daughter of Sir Henry and Margaret Cholmeley, was married to the Hon. and Rev. Henry Fairfax, son of the first Lord Fairfax of Denton, and she appears to have carried this book with her to her new home.

Being a clergyman, her husband evidently prized the volume very highly, as he would be frequently called upon to minister to the sick. After their marriage he made large additions to it in his own characteristic handwriting, and Mary also entered in it her private collection of receipts for baking meats, bleaching yarn, and other homely arts. A clue to the date of Henry's earlier writings is found on page 74, where reference is made to Ell. Fairfax. This niece of his became Lady Selby shortly after 1630, and there is the strongest probability that this portion was written previous to her marriage. There is also on page 135 a recipe dated Feb. 25, 1632, which he may have obtained from Lady Fairfax at Steeton, on his return journey from London, whither he had gone a few weeks previously. Henry was assiduous in his search for medical knowledge, and doubtless, while the first heat of his enthusiasm lasted, made himself a bore to all his relations. His brother-in-law, Henry Cholmeley, was the possessor of a similar book, and from this he seems largely to have borrowed, always, however, acknowledging the source of his receipt by adding the initials H. C. His brother, Sir Ferdinando Fairfax, had married a daughter of Lord Sheffield, and he ransacked Lady Sheffield's book, which at that time was in the hands of Sir Ferdinando's married daughter, Mrs. Dorothy Hutton. His numerous cousins were importuned for contributions, and his almost countless nieces were in turn called upon to swell the volume. Occasionally someone contributed a receipt in his own hand, as Henry Cholmeley (page 56), Sir Ferdinando Fairfax (page 146), and others unknown. How long this process of collection continued on the part of the Rev. Henry Fairfax is not easy to determine, but there is some probability that his son Brian wrote some pages (151-3) in it about the time of the great plague in London.

The Book seems to have passed at Henry's death into the possession of his elder son Henry, fourth Lord Fairfax of Denton, whose daughter Ann, following the example of her grandmother, Mary Cholmeley, probably carried it to her new home when she married Ralph Carr, Esq., of Cocken,

in the County of Durham. Her son Ralph, who was born
in 1694, and married to Margaret Paxton in 1721, does not
seem to have valued the book so highly as did the Fairfaxes,
because either he or his son Ralph presented it as a gift (pages
1 and 206) to his neighbour Robert Green of Cocken, whom
as yet I have been unable to trace. The Carrs were
connected by marriage with the Hodgsons of Hebborne, and
the Davisons of North Biddick, they in turn, as well as the
Hedworths, being related to the families of Bellasis and
Penniman of previous generations, who were kinsfolk of the
Fairfaxes, and all of whom are mentioned in the "Arcana."
These neighbours round about Cocken, although historically
less prominent than the Fairfax group of the previous century,
are highly interesting to the North Country from their
intimate relationship to its notable families, the Delavals
of Seaton, the Lambtons of Lambton, the Liddells of
Ravensworth, the Hedworth-Williamsons of Monkwearmouth
and Whitburn, the Carr-Ellisons, the Fenwicks, the Forsters,
and many more almost equally illustrious.

Robert Green seems to have been a man after Henry
Fairfax's own heart, as he levied literary black mail upon his
friends for many miles, besides proving and recommending the
recipes with hearty zeal. We have no record as to the time
when much of this section was written, although in the

index at the end of the book (page 194) we see that Mr. Hedworth (who was M.P. for Durham at the time) sent down from London a recipe for an ague in 1728. Almost the last entry in the book gives a clue to the date when it was written. On page 190 we find some specifics copied from "Mr. Blackrie's treatise, *just published.*" This Mr. Blackrie was an Apothecary, who, in 1763, contributed a paper to the "Scots Magazine," in which he exposed the secret of Dr. Chittick's cure for gravel. In 1766 he expanded his letter into a volume, and he died in 1772. It is probable, therefore, that page 190 and the following, which are the latest additions to the volume, were written between 1766 and 1770.

The Fairfax Family.

One account gives the Fairfaxes a Northumbrian origin, with a seat at Towcester in that county at or before the Conquest. The name is Saxon, and signifies "fair hair." They were certainly settled in Yorkshire about the beginning of the 13th century. Since that time they have been a very notable Yorkshire family, and have on several occasions exerted a powerful influence in forming the history of England. Sir Guy Fairfax, a Judge of the Court of King's

Bench in 1478, built a castle at Steeton, which became the principal residence of the family. Sir William Fairfax of Steeton, heir to Sir Guy, became a Judge of the Common Pleas; and *his* heir Sir William, was High Sheriff of York in the reign of Henry VIII., and by marriage obtained the manor of Denton.

This latter Sir William having ample means, divided his property between his two eldest sons, Sir Thomas and Gabriel, thus dividing the family into two branches, the Fairfaxes of Denton, and the Fairfaxes of Steeton. The former has occupied the greater place in history, but the latter only is still in, Yorkshire, at Bilbrough, where there has been a seat of the family for three-and-a-half centuries.

Sir Thomas Fairfax, of Denton, had a younger son Edward, a poet, and the translator of Tasso. Both Sir Thomas and his heir of the same name were eminent diplomatists in the time of Queen Elizabeth, the younger having been five times sent into Scotland to treat with King James. This second Sir Thomas, who became the first Lord Fairfax, had nine children, of whom four sons were killed in war abroad, and three others, Ferdinando, Charles, and Henry, are worthy of separate note.

Ferdinando (second Lord Fairfax) was one of the prominent leaders of the great Revolution, both in camp and council. He was a member of the Long Parliament, and was appointed commander of the ¡northern forces. He married Lady Mary Sheffield, and had nine or ten children, several of whom are mentioned in the "Arcana."

Charles was a lawyer, as well as a soldier, and wrote on vellum an interesting genealogical work entitled "Analecta Fairfaxiana" containing an exhaustive history of the family. I have not been fortunate enough to see this book, but a little further on I have drawn up a pedigree of the Denton Fairfaxes for several generations, showing the relationship that existed between a number of the persons mentioned. I also print in full Henry's note of his nephews and nieces, the latter portion referring to the Cholmeley side ; and finally there is a list of the names in this book, with their relationship or notability stated opposite to each.

Henry Fairfax, who is the centre of interest as far as the book is concerned, was rector of Ashton, then of Newton Kyme, and afterwards of Bolton Percy, near York. As already stated, he married Mary, daughter of Sir Henry Cholmeley of Whitby, a family scarcely less notable than that of the Fairfaxes. Before their marriage in 1626, they were devotedly attached to each other, but, owing to their portionless condition, their union seemed hopeless. Mary, writing to her "assured loving cousin, Harry Fairfax," fears

that "we may both wish you had not thought me worthy
of the title of dear love," but "so dear you are in my
esteem, as I assure you you have no cause to doubt the
continuance of my firm affection;" and she adds, "I will
wear your ring until you take it from me." They were
married, however, in 1626, and in 1632 we find her writing
to London, whither her husband had gone on a journey:

"My ever dearest love,

I received a letter and horse from long on Thrusday
(Jan. 31), and will use meine (endeavour) to send Procter's
horse to Denton. I did nott so much rejoys att thy safe
passage as at that Bleised and al suficiente gide whoss thou
art, and whom I know thou truely sarves, yᵗ hath for a small
time parted us, and I fearmly hope will give us a joyfull
meeting. Dear hart, take eassy jernays and preferr thy
owne heilth before all other worldly respects whatsoever.
Thy three boys at Ashton are well, thy little Harry is
weaned, all that love us pray for thy safe return. I pray
yᵘ beg a blessing for us all, for I must needs comitt yᵘ to
his gracious protection, yᵗ will never fail us nor forsake us.

"Thine ever,

"MARY FAIRFAX."

"Ashton, Feb. 2nd, 1632."

The "Little Harry" mentioned in this touching letter was their third child, but the two elder died when young, and he became fourth Lord Fairfax on the death of his cousin Thomas, third Lord and Parliamentary General, who had only one child, Mary, married to the Duke of Buckingham.

The married life of Henry and Mary Fairfax seems to have been peculiarly sympathetic. Henry's gentle disposition, no less than his sacred calling, prevented him from taking any part in the political troubles of the time, which divided almost every great family in England. To quote from an entry in the Fairfax MSS., "All the time of the civil wars, from 1642 to 1646, their little parsonage was a refuge and a sanctuary to all their friends and relations on both sides." Mary, who was delicate, and it appears somewhat lame, died in 1649, and was buried in Bolton Percy Church. Henry died in 1665, and was buried in the same place, "near to his dear wife."

During the Civil War the Fairfaxes were perhaps the most powerful family on the side of the Parliament. Henry's brothers Ferdinando (then second Lord Fairfax) and Charles held important commands, the former being the General of the Parliament in the first Yorkshire campaign and commanding the right wing of the allied army at the battle of Marston Moor. Sir Thomas, eldest son of Ferdinando, and the most celebrated of all the Fairfaxes, was appointed Commander-in-

Chief of the army by votes of the two Houses of Parliament, and it was due mainly to his resolute and skilful marshalling that the Parliamentary forces were ultimately triumphant. It is he whom Milton addresses in his sonnet, "To the Lord General Fairfax," beginning—

> "Fairfax, whose name in arms through Europe rings,
> Filling each mouth with envy or with praise."

Notwithstanding the prominent part he played in the Revolution, he was a man of moderate views, and only fought against the king through a stern sense of duty to his country. He resolutely opposed the extreme party when they proposed to execute the unhappy monarch, and by every means in his power, short of violence, sought to prevent or delay the last act. He was afterwards largely instrumental in the restoration of the monarchy, whose atrocities and excesses, however, he lived to mourn and abhor.

His two cousins, Henry and Brian, sons of the Rev. Henry Fairfax, were frequently guests in his house at Nunappleton during his latter years, and the former succeeded him as the fourth Lord Fairfax. Brian played rather an important part in the Restoration, and recounts in a little book entitled "Iter Boreale," his adventures during a perilous journey in mid-winter from York to Kelso, to consult with General Monk. He was a poet of considerable merit, and

might have further distinguished himself in the literary art had
he been sufficiently serious to apply himself assiduously to any
one pursuit. He wrote a memoir of the Duke of Buckingham,
and translated the life of Philip Mornay, Seigneur du Plessis.
He was equerry to Charles II. from 1670 until that king's
death, and afterwards to William III. He acted as secretary
to his old friend Archbishop Tillotson for three years, and
died in 1711.

Henry, the fourth Lord, left, with other children,
two sons—Thomas, who succeeded as fifth Lord, and Henry
whose son William settled in Virginia, and is the ancestor
of the American Fairfaxes. William's son Brian, the friend
of Washington, afterwards succeeded as eighth Lord, and
his descendants all live in America (Markham's " Life of
Fairfax.") The eleventh Lord resides in Maryland, U.S.A.,
and has graduated as a Doctor of Medicine.

The Fairfaxes, of Steeton, the second great branch of
the family, has had its warriors on sea and land. Sir William,
cousin to the great general, died gallantly at Montgomery
Castle while leading his troops to victory. His son William,
who married the niece of Sir Philip Stapleton, had a son,
Robert, who commanded a ship at the taking of Gibraltar,
and became a vice-admiral in 1707. His descendants now
reside at Bilbrough, which has been a seat of the Fairfaxes
since the time of Henry VIII.

Genealogical Table of the Fairfaxes.

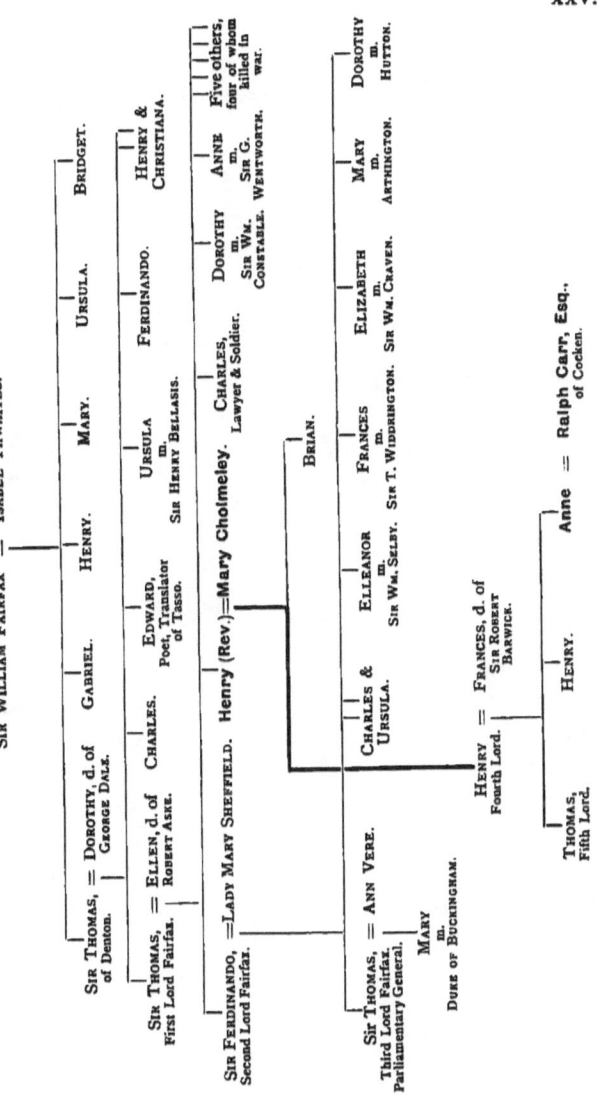

Nephews and Nieces of H. and M. F.

"A NOTE OF SUCH NEPHEWES AND NEECES AS ARE OR
WERE ALLYED TO US, H. & M.F."

FEB. 10, 1635.

(BRIT. MUS., ADD. MSS. 11,325, FOL. 48).

Sir Fer. Fairfax, his 9 children .	9
Mr. Charles Fairfax . .	7
Mr. Thos. Widdrington .	1
Mr. Richard Hutton .	1
Sir Geo. Wentworth's . . .	1
	—
	19

Sir Hugh Cholmeley and his Ladyes had	9
Barbary, ye La. Bellasis had	11
Dorothy Bushell . .	14
Hilda Wright . .	5
Margaret Comin . .	16
Susa Theakeston .	7
Annabella Wickham . .	4
	—
	66

	66
Sir Hugh Cholmeley (Sup.) his Lady and 5 children . .	6
Mr. He. Bellasis, his Lady and 7 children	8
Sir Ed. Osborne and 2 children	3
John, Lord Darcy and 1 child .	2
Sir Hen. Hugesby and 1 child	2
Brown Bushell's wife and 2 children	3
He. Bushell's wife and 1 child .	2
Mr. Conyers and 7 children .	8
Mr. Dobson and 3 children.	4
Mr. Newton and 5 children .	6
Sir Wm. Strickland and 3 children	4
Mr. Trotter and 2 children .	3
My La. Twisleton, by Sir Hen. Cholmeley	1
	—
	118

Fairfax and Forster.

It may interest north country people to note the relationship between these two families. Elleanor Fairfax, daughter of Lord Ferdinando Fairfax was married to Sir William Selby of Twizell, and was the Lady Selby mentioned in the "Arcana." Her daughter Dorothy was married to Sir William Forster of Bamburgh, whose daughter Dorothy was married to Lord Crewe, and was the aunt of the younger "Dorothy Forster" of Mr. Besant's romance.

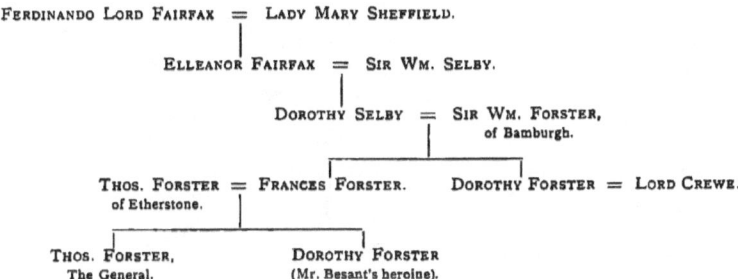

Sir William Forster had a son Ferdinando, named after Lord Fairfax, who was killed in Newcastle by a member of one of the neighbouring families.

Seventeenth Century Names.

Eighteenth Century Names.

The Handwritings.

In giving specimens of some of the handwritings, I have not arranged them according to their position in the volume, because the large gaps left between the sections by the original writers, allowed later comers to interject stray receipts, and even small collections. They are arranged according to the periods when they were written. First, there is the "Cholmeley" period, including all writings previous to the marriage of Mary Cholmeley to Henry Fairfax in 1626; second, the "Fairfax period from 1626 to 1660 or 1670; third, the "Green" period, relating only to the 18th century writings, its utmost limit being from 1730 to 1770.

Having already brought the earlier writings to a period after 1600, I shall not be misunderstood when I give comparative examples of similar hands dated prior to this. The exact dating of a manuscript from the handwriting alone is very difficult. The "Court" hand of one age might linger on in the country districts, and be taught by old people (who were generally the schoolmasters and schooldames) fifty years after the time when they themselves had learned to write. Or the "Law" hand might show a conservative tendency, and retain an ancient character long after the literary or other classes had adopted a more convenient style. Hence, without knowing the location, profession, or standing of the writer, the handwriting only brings us to within fifty years or so of the date when it was written. I shall not, therefore, attempt to fix a date to any of the earlier hands, but give examples of their occurrence elsewhere, so that those readers desirous of doing so may have the pleasure of comparison and criticism.

I.—The "Shakespearian" Hand.

(Page 3).

(Page 98).

id est (Page 3).

"How to use my hopes [hops] and hop-garthe, being sett.
"In october digg the hop-yard betweene the hills and rid the diches
  "[ditches] round about, so lett yt lye all the wynter tyll marche
  "lyke a fallow ground, but styrr not the hills tyll marche."

(Page 98).

"Steepe one-dram-and-a-half of Ruberb one whole night in six
  "ounces of whay, wringe yt out the next morninge and drinck
  "that whay at six of the clock that same morninge, fastinge
  "tyll X° and at a XI dyne wth som p[ar]t of a henn stewed,
  "but drinck a draught of the water wherin the henn ys stodd,
  "before y^u putt any bread or freut into the broth."

I call this the "Shakespearian" hand because it
occurs in the Stratford and many other records of the time
of Shakespeare and his father. Good examples of it in
that earlier form may be found in the "Outlines of the
Life of Shakespeare," by the late Mr. Halliwell-Phillips,
and in "Shakespearian Facsimiles," by the same author. In
the seventh edition of the former work, vol. II., fol. 236,
is an excellent specimen showing how John Shakespeare, the
poet's father, was replaced as an Alderman of his Guild
because he "Dothe not come to the Halles when they be
warned, nor hathe not done of longe tyme."

A much later development of the style is seen in
the "Percy Folio," from where Bishop Percy largely culled
in 1765 his "Reliques of Ancient English Poetry." This
manuscript, which is exhibited in the British Museum, is

supposed to have been written about the middle of the 17th century; but the writing is more characteristic of an earlier part of the century, and was probably done by someone past middle life. A specimen of it may be seen fac-similed in "Bishop Percy's Folio Ballads and Romances," published by Trubner and Co., in 1867. Careful comparison of this will show that the letters f, g, h, k, s, t, also st, and th, are generally of a more modern character than those of the examples in this book. A hand almost exactly similar to that on page 3 of the "Arcana" is found in the British Museum, Add. MSS. 30,305, fol. 19. It was written by Thomas Wynter, in 1606, and consists of "A Collection of the Earll of North[umberland] his cause, on his alleged complicity in the Gunpowder Plot."

II.—The "Secretary" Hand.

(Page 117.)

id est

"TO CRAMME CAPONS.

"Take ffine wheate meale and mingle itt wth suger or honney and
"soe make itt into Rowles, and soe you may make a capon
"fatt in six dayes. But the wheate meale must be moulded
"wth Butter or Sewette."

This is the more official style of the time of Elizabeth
and onwards. In the Sloan MS. No. 1832 and the Harleian
No. 3885 we find writing masters of Elizabeth's time calling
it the "Secretarye hannde," Long after this, William Fairfax
uses it in writing to his brother Henry at Trinity College,
Cambridge. Even so late as 1660 it was taught to schoolboys,
and was then known, I think, as "Henry VIII. writing."

III.—The "Glossyng" Hand.

(Page 124.)

id est

"HOW TO DY A FRENCH GRENE.

"First make it a good blewe, then wash it up in faire water,
"then taike allome according to the p[ro]portion, and boyle
"it thre houres alwaies when you use any allome; then taike
"it up, then taike faire water and grene grasse and boyle them
"an houre togith' then taike out your grene," &c.

Although this differs so widely in effect from the
hands I. and II., there are many examples in the British
Museum which seem transitions between I. and III., and
between II. and III. Thus the MS. 17 A. vi., which is
of the 16th century, has the characteristics of I. and III.
combined, being more finely written than the former, but
of distinctly earlier hand than the latter. The nearest

approach to the "Glossyng" hand which I have seen occurs in the Add. MS. 30,305, fol. 17, which was written in 1600 by "Ra Fure."

IV.—The "Italian" Hand.

(Page 14.)

For the swyming in ye head: guien by m^r Vessalius (ye Emperor Charles phisition) to Quene Mary:

Take two ounces of the iuice of the budds of redd roses or one ounce of very good oile of roses, one ounce of kowslip oile, and two spoonefulls of womans milk of a manchild, and three nutmegs fynely beaten &c sereed and asmuch mace made in powder as the nutmegs is, and a little red rose water, and asmuch tyme (v miger; mingle all these togeather and swarme it (ppon a Chasingdish, and anointe the nape of the neck and the temples, and the crowne of the head, and (nder ye eares you must rub it (veary (vell in, and keepe the head (vholl (vhile it is a dompe and after:

This was not a common hand in England until about 1615, when the London writing masters Richard Gething, John Ayres, and others taught it to their pupils. Abroad, however, in Italy and in France, it was quite common as early as 1550 (MSS. 14 a. xvi., &c.) It was also taught in England by Teshe, of York, and others of Temp. Eliz., who called it the "Italique hannde," (origin of our *Italics*) but it was regarded as distinctly foreign, and was only used in continental languages. The MS. 17 A. vii., for instance, begins in the Italian hand, the language written being French; it continues in the Secretary hand, in English; and again reverts to the Italian, written this time in the Italian language. The best specimen of this writing which I have seen is the Sloan MS. 987, written in 1586 by a young French Lady residing in Edinburgh, Esther Langlois (elsewhere called Anglois and Inglis). The style of writing used in Italy, however, in the beginning of the 17th century was more cursive than this, somewhat like that of Charles Fairfax's hand, or in a much less degree of his brother Henry, which is shown in the style V. This lends some support to the idea that the younger Fairfaxes were taught by their uncle Edward, the poet, who, as translator of Tasso, was certain to be acquainted with the Italian Schools and methods.

V.—Henry Fairfax's Writing.

(Page 140.)

id est
"FOR Yᴱ KING'S EVILL.

"R. [take] Folefoot [coltsfoot] stamped with his rootes, yᵉ flowre
"of yᵉ seeds of Lyne or flax and yᵉ grease of a Barrow-hogge,
"mixe them all together, make thereof a plaster and lay it
"upon yᵉ soare, changing it twice a day, and all yᵉ sores of
"yᵉ desease will be resolved into sweat. After they be healed
"wash often yᵉ place with white wine by yᵉ space of 10 or
"15 days."

"HOW TO KNOW Yᴱ K[ING'S] EVILL.

"Take a ground worme alive and lay him upon yᵉ swelling or sore
"and cover him with a leafe. Yf it be yᵉ disease yᵉ worme
"will change and turn into earth. Yf it be not he will remain
"whole and sound."

VI.—Mary (Cholmeley) Fairfax's Writing.
(Page 120.)

to make puffe past

138.

Take a quantety of fine flower
4 whits of eggs. a little rose water
or other cold watter; mold ye paste
together & beat it ws ye rollinpin; for
ye stiffer ye make it ye better

id est
"TO MAKE PUFFE PASTE.

"Take a quantety of fine flower, 4 whits of Eggs, a little rose
"water or other cold water; mold your paste together and
"beat it with your rollin-pin for yᵉ stiffer yᵘ make it, yᵉ
"better."

VII.—Brian Fairfax's Writing.

(Page 151.)

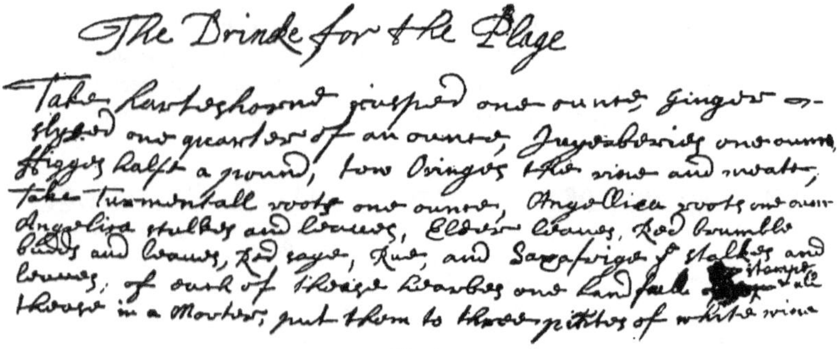
The Drinke for the Plage

Take hartshorne rasped one ounce, ginger slysed one quarter of an ounce, Juyesberies one ounce, ffigges halfe a pound, tow Oringes the rine and meate, take Turmentall roots one ounce, Angellica roots one ounce Angellica stalkes and leaves, Elder leaves, Red bramble budds and leaves, Red sage, Rue, and Saxafrige ye stalkes and leaves, of each of these hearbes one handfull stamped all these in a Morter, put them to three pinttes of white wine

id est

"THE DRINKE FOR THE PLAGE.

"Take hartshorne rasped one ounce, ginger slysed, one quarter "of an ounce, Juyes-beries [goose-berries] one ounce, ffigges "half a pound, tow (2) oringes, the rind and meate. Take "Turmentall roots one ounce, angellica roots one ounce, "angellica stalkes and leaves, Elder leaves, Red bramble "budds and leaves, Red sage, Rue and Saxafrige ye stalkes "and leaves, of each of these hearbes one handful, stamped "all," etc.

182 Syrup of Clove July 8 Coors ·

Take half pound of Cloors put 'ym into a pott
& power 9 gills of Boyling water upon 'ym cover it
& lett it Stand 3 or 4 hours then Strain it through
a seive & put two pound of Loaf Sug — to one pint
& Give a boill or two & Scum it very well —
you may clear it up wth whites of Egg

IX.—**Nineteenth Century.**

Handwriting as an art, will probably, in the course of
next century, be superseded by the more legible Type-writer,
and the still more convenient phonograph. I therefore add, for
the enlightenment of the readers of the next century, a specimen
of the present style of writing :—

In the prospectus first issued, this work was
entitled "Ye Apothecarie his booke"; but
failing to discover evidence of its having
been used by an Apothecary, the name was
altered to "Areane Fairfaxiana"
on account of its owners & writers.

The Subject Matter.

Medical Recipes.

To describe the herbs and simples used in the medical receipts would be congenial labour, and in undertaking it I should be more at home than in what I have already attempted. But that would fill a volume in itself, and would not be generally interesting to the book lover. I shall therefore only make brief reference to the subject matter, leaving the rest to the leisurely perusal of the reader.

The collections found between pages 9—58, and 75—96, although written in the same Italian hand, were evidently culled from different sources. The second, at least, seems copied from an Apothecary's book, the first may have been also. The other writings of that period, such as those on pages 96 and 97 also bear the marks of professional skill. The renowned " weapon-salve " of Paracelsus, mentioned on page 61, although still recommended by his disciple Dr. Fludd in 1606, had almost fallen into disrepute as a professional remedy, partly on acconnt of the ban of the Church, partly from the increased enlightenment of the medical men. Almost the only auxiliary to physical remedies was the reverent invocation of " God's grace ;" and in spite of occasional appeals to the imagination, in the form of charms or talismans, the " Cholmeley " writing may be said to represent the professional method of the time.

The " Fairfax " receipts, while still dealing in charms, exhibit a greater number of remedies in which diet and régime are the chief factors. They represent, therefore, domestic rather than professional medicine, and are just what would be used by families residing at some distance from the towns.

The medical portion of the " Green " collection, as might be expected from its later date, shows a great advance in the evolution of scientific treatment. The remedies generally have become more definite, and are often chosen as on page 221 with a single and rational end in view. Cures for the bite of a mad dog are not effected by a " Hair of the dog that bit you," but by means which might have been used up to within a very recent date. This is said, however, with all respect for the more ancient treatment, for does not the method of M. Pasteur after all consist in a homœopathically diluted " Microbe of the dog that bit you ? "

Housewifery.

The Sections devoted to the household arts form a large proportion of the book, and although bleaching and dyeing, brewing and preserving, are now almost entirely relegated to the manufacturer, the baking of meats still continues to engage the attention of the housewife. It may therefore be interesting to some fair readers to try the methods of those ancient dames, for the food upon which such noble men were reared in the days of Queen Bess and of the Commonwealth, may still be capable of making healthy bone and brain and blood. A crammed capon followed by pancakes made with cream—only think of it! (*See* recipe, page 117.)

Touches of Nature.

Here and there, throughout the book, there are evidences of the same human nature which is the heritage of all time. Some one, finding it convenient for her purpose, scribbles on page 60 the copy of a letter written to some "Right noble Knight," asking him for a stag which she wishes to send to London, invoking Harry Cholmeley as a mutual acquaintance. The writer of the Italian hand, perhaps resident in the household but not a member of the family, enters on the last page "A note of Miss Barbara, her lessons on y⁶ virginalle, which she hath learned and can play them." On the same page a watchful housewife notes the contents of her poultry yard as follows: "i kapon, xvi Torkies, xviii dowkes, iiii henes, ii cokes, x chekins, x giese, iv sowes, ii brawes, [? brawnes].

There is also on page 201 a record of lost linen, including handkerchares, fallenge bandes of kambreke, and other articles. Near at hand, on page 200 reversed, some masculine penman has copied a charm "To stanch the bleeding at the nose," which deserves to be given in full, as it may prove of assistance to those who in the present day put a key down the back of the person so affected. It is written in "latin" *sic*—

> "Sanguis manet in te,
> "Sicut Christus ferat in se,
> "Sanguis manet in tua vena,
> "Sicut Christus in sua pena;
> "Sanguis manet in te fixus,
> "Sicut Christus in Crussifixus.

> "Say this over three times, naming the partyes nam, and then say the Lord's Prayer."

These "asides" are not the least interesting feature of the book, They show that it has passed through many hands,—that the hopeful maiden as well as the lean apothecary, the anxious housewife as well as the learned divine, the equerry of Charles the Second's court, and the country squire of a century later, all had a hand in its making, adding something of interest to them and to us. They also enable us more readily to call up the family life of those interesting days in or about 1600, when My Lady Cholmeley, having ordered her household during the morning, and instructed her many daughters in their xlvi.

various duties, went round her domain from hop-garthe to hen-
yard, from linen closet to larder, prying, tasting, and admonishing,
until her family was called together to "dyne at XI. of the
clocke." And later in the day, when Henry and John had
gone out with their father to shoot, and while Mary and Hilda
and Dorothy were instructed, as was the custom in all noble
families, in the arts of reading and writing, Mistress Barbara,
being now nigh twenty years old, played her lessons on the
virginal, thinking all the while of young Thomas Bellasis, who
would ere long come in with her brothers, and who would
praise the singing of her latest lessons, " My trew loue is to y°
Grene wood gon."

The Reproduction, and How it was Done.

When first considering the publication of the manuscript, I was uncertain whether it ought to be printed in letterpress with merely a few specimens of the handwriting in fac-simile, or entirely in fac-simile as now produced. The former would appeal to a larger class, because many persons might read in type what in the original manuscript would be tedious and difficult ; yet to the genuine book-worm a little difficulty or even utter unintelligibility in some portions would be an additional fascination. The publishers having put before me the possibilities of production in either fashion, I decided to address the book to the latter class, and publish it in fac-simile throughout. Should they or others desire an edition in letterpress, the publishers and the writer will be pleased to receive their suggestions.

The method of reproduction now had to be decided, the choice lying between tracing the entire volume by hand or copying it by photography. The latter would have been by far the easier process had the book been in good condition and clean, but after experiment it was decided to adopt the former, bringing in the aid of photography here and there, xlviii.

where practicable. The reproduction by hand was so successful, however, being in most instances indistinguishable from the original except by the colour of the paper, that photography was only sparingly employed, and the pages so copied (see between 108—135) have been marked in the volume. The printing has been done by the lithographic process. There is some pleasure in stating that a high authority in manuscripts in the British Museum considers the fac-simile "most successful."

Every line of the Work has been compared with the original, and where the slightest deviation was found it has been corrected or retraced. The only features not attempted in the reproduction are, the stains on the paper—although all the blots have been copied where they do not too greatly interfere with legibility,—and the various shades of the faded ink, which indicate more clearly in the original manuscript where some writer has added a comment on the work of his predecessor.

George Windsor

2, *Stannington Avenue,*
Newcastle-on-Tyne,
November 17th, 1890.

The Manuscript
in Fac=simile.

Ursula   Rob\. Green
Cocker

ursula Lister

Henry

Hen Fairfax

Ro. Green. Cocken. Ex Dono. R. C.

Si Vis curari de morbo nescio quali.
Accipias Herbam, sed quale nescio, nec quã;
Zonas, nescio quò; curaberis, nescio quando.
&c&c.

Your Sore, & know not What, doe not fore slow
To cure wth Herbs; Which, Whence I doe not know.
Place them (well pounc't) I know not Where; as then
You shall be perfect Whole, & know not When.

To make good inck

Take a quart of Rayne water, or Clarett
wyne, or... vinegar not being too sharp
5 ounces of gall / 4 ounces of Copperas /
3 ounces of Gume / beat y... gall and
Copperas a... to 2... of the water
... lett... stand... make the
Gume would be put in...
after 5 days standing... then a
little but beware ... the longer
... wile ... it ... put in a...
...

~~To make~~ Take a Quart of fair Spring-Water, one ounce of Copperas, 2 ounces of Gall, &
4 ounces of Gume Arabick, mingle the together & lett thes stand.   *Mr Midgeley*

Take 4 ounces of Gume arabick beat small, 2 ounces of Gall beat groß,
one ounce of Copperas, & 1 quart of y comeing off of strong Ale, putt all
theise together, & stirre them 3 or 4 times a day about 14 days. Then
strein it through a cloath.   *Mr Dockwey.*

I made Ink by ye above rect only puting half
ye arabick and as good as ever was up
N: Green

Mr Mason Exciseman his rect for
making Ink, which is very good
Take a Quart of Rain or other Soft water
And put to it 4 oz of galls grosly beatten brustleu
let it stand warm for 3 days Then add 2 oz of Copperas
4 oz of Gum, Ditto allam let it stand 2 or 3 days longer
best shake it up 2 or 3 times a day put a little brandy into

4

6

Ano̅: signesyte of weig̅t a like weight or Quantity.
lib. a pownd the weighth. — (or a quart) — — — — ℥ 12.
lib. ß. half a pownd. (lib ß) (or a pinte — — — ℥ 6.
℥i· one ōu̅ce (℥i) — — — — 3 8.
℥ß. half an ōu̅ce (℥ß) — — — — 3 4.
3·j· one drea̅m (3j is 3 3. or) — — — — gr. 60
3· ß· half a drea̅m (3 ß) — — — — gr. 30.
Ʒj· one scru̅pule (Ʒj) — — — gr. 20.
Ʒ ß· half a scru̅pull (Ʒ ß) — — — gr. 10.
m: signesyte a greyne weig̅t.
manipule. a hendfull.
4 mille. weyt one way gold between the
two hee fingers a the thombe.
m̅: sandes, for argent nob e gr̅ please./

Note. A graine is a Barly-corne.
a Scruple is 20 graines
3. Scruples a Drāme.
8 Drāmes an Ounce.
12 Ounces a Pound.

For a Wenn

Take a quantity of black soape and so much good ginger, made into
fine powder, and mix ye same with soape like vnto a thick salue.
Then lay it plaster wise vppon a peece of fine new white cloth
or rather leather, pricked full of holes: Lett ye plaister so rest
vppon the sore 12 or 24 howers. according as you shall feele it
to worke: and then chaunge and renew it accordingly. Contineu
and renew this plaster euery day vntill ye sore do break. wch
wilbe within xv daies: and still contineu ye plaister after ye
sore is broken vntill ye sore be as flatt and as lowe, as any other
parte of ye flesh: Do not cutt or prick ye sore, but lett it break
by ye working of ye medicine: Make no more medycine at once
then will serue for a weeke, and then weekly make fresh. /
When ye corruption is cleane drawen forth, then will apeare to
remaine the bagg or skynn of the Wenn, vnto which applie
nothing. but yor fasting spittle first forseeing all ye corruption
to be veary cleane drawen forth: Deuise some cleauing thinge
about ye edges of the plaster, broder then shall touche ye soare
therby to make ye plaster to abide vpon ye sore wch otherwise
yt cannot because ye soape is slippery and not cleauinge :/ ———

For ye same.
Take May-butter well clarifyed in ye sunne, Broome-budds, Durtrea
flowers, Violet-leaues, red-Sage & a litle-Camomile.

qn Bering

For the reddnes of the eyes or bludshod

Take redd wine, redrose water and womans milk, and mingle all
these togeather, and cutt a peece of y crommes of wheaten bread
leuened, asmuch as will couer the eie; and laye it in the red wine.
rose water and milke, and when you go to bedd, laye it vppon your
eies and it will help them. ꝛꝛꝛꝛ—

For Chilblanes & Kibes

Take faire water and wheat branne, and seeth it till it be very soft
and laye it vppon the place greeued so whot as you can suffer yt
and if it be broken it will heale it; and if it be not broken it will
aswage it. ꝛꝛꝛ—

For an ache in any parte of y bodye. ꝛꝛꝛ

Take two or three onions: pill them and slice them & beate them smale
and putt therto in sponefulls of sallett oile and asmuch aquacomposita
stamp them well togeather, strame them thorough a cloth, then
take it, warme it whott and anointe y greeued place, and warm: a
cloth, and it on it. ꝛꝛꝛ—

For y̗ bleeding at y̗ nose : Probatum X

Take a Toade and drie it in marche put y̗ same into some silke
or sattene bagg and hange it about y̗ neck of y̗ party next the
skinne and by gods grace it will stanch presently : //

For the falling sicknes

Take the harte of a toade and drie it and beate it to powder, then
drinke with what drinke you will : ⁓⁓⁓

A psent medicine for a laske ⁓⁓
as is good for bleeding. y̗

Take a Toade at any tyme of y̗ yere and drie it in an ouen, so it doth
not breake and when it is dried putt it into some taffaty bagg and
hange it about y̗ necke of y̗ party greeued next y̗ skin : it helpeth

For a Pynn and Webb : //

Take a handfull of hemlock and y̗ white of an egge and a little haysalt
altogeather (veary fine & lay it to y̗ pulce of y̗ arme on y̗ contrary side
and if it be nere y̗ sight of y̗ eie to y̗ iuce of dases leaues rootes & all
and put it into y̗ eie, and so vse it, till it be whole . ⁓⁓⁓

For swelling of ame parte

Take Kamomill flovers, and if you cannot gett ỹ flovers, take ỹ
herbs and take newe milke, and put ỹ herbs into yt, and barlie
meale if you can gett no barly meale, take otmeale and seeth all
these in ỹ milke togeather, till yt be thick, and then laie it on ỹ
swellinp place, so hot as ỹ patient can indure it, and in twice
vsinp ỹ same, it will ridd yt awaye ∙ // ∽

For the shrinkinp of ỹ sinewes ∙

Take a pinte of neatsfoote oile, and half a pound of may butter, &
half a pound of sowes grease, smalledg ℩ mallowes of ỹ field ℩
& of french mallowes hafe a pound ∶ chop all these verie smale
togeather, then boile it in the same butter and grease aforesayd ∙
Vntill it be half boiled awaye, then strame it and anoint ỹ place
warminp it first, both eueninp and morninp ∙ and it will help it ∙ //

Anoyntment for the Palsye.

Take the flowers of s Tickades, the flowers of y right spike, the flowers
of french lauender, the flowers and cropps of rosemary, y flowers &
cropps of Isop; y flowers and crops of maudline, and a handfull of
kowslipp flowers, y crops of sage, of each of them a handfull, and of
Camomill flowers, three handfuls : put them all into sallet oile, and
make it as you make oile of Roses. y

For them theyr speech faileth. \

Take a handfull of y cropps of Rosemary, a handfull of sage, and a
handfull of Isop and boile them in malmsey, till it be soft, then
put them into lynen clothes, and laye about the nape of the neck
and the pulses of the armes, as whott as it may be suffred, daily,
as it shalbe thought mete, and it will help it, by gods grace.

For the same :

Take Stauesaker and beate it, and sowe it in a linnen cloth, and make
a bagg, noe bigger then a beane, if he can chow it in his mouth, lett
hym, if not then lay it vppon his teunge.

For y'e Palsey that draweth y'e sinowes.

Take kowslip rootes and seeth them in malmsey, and bathe them
therewith where he is drawen, and strike to y'e right place, as warme
as may be suffred, and if he cannot speake, rubb his tongue w'th newe
masterd and pepper, or els with y'e same medicine aforesaide
made of staues acre, or with aquacomposita and herbgrace, and
mingle it togeather, & rub y'e nape of y'e neck w'th it, & so vnder y'e eares.

For the swyming in y'e head, giuen by m'r Vesalius
(y'e Emperor Charles phisition) to Quene Mary:

Take two ounces of the iuice of the budds of redd roses or one ounce of
very good oile of roses, one ounce of kowslip oile, and two spoonefulls
of womans milk of a manchild and three nutmegs finely beaten &
serced and asmuch mace made in powder as the nutmegs is, and a little
red rose water and asmuch wine vineger; mingle all these togeather
and warme it vppon a Chafingdish, and anointe the nape of the
neck and the temples, and the crowne of the head, and vnder y'e eares
you must rub it veary well in, and keepe the head whott while it is
a doinge and after.

8·57
4ᵗ·44.

For the paine in the back.

Take a quart of new milke from the Cowe, and the briskit of a
brest of mutton, cutt of ẙ skinne and all the fatt as nere as you
can, and bente y bones, and putt into the milk (without washing
it; Take nyne leaues of clary, and nine leaues of nepp; and a
good handfull of knottgrace, and nine leaues of comfory; putt
all these into the milk (with the mutton, and lett it boile halfe
awaye; bruse a nutineg, and put it in, and let it seeth a waume
or two after, and then strainé it, and lett it stand till it be could
skim of ẙ fatt & warme it & drinke euery morne & euen a draught

Another for the same.

Take three leaues of Nepp, and fiue leaues of Clary and
three leaues of Comforyé and the pithe of the oxe back
and chopp all these togeather, and frye (with a cupple of egos
in sweete butter, and eate it euery morninge, and a little before
you eate it drinke a little draught of muskadell, and an other
draught after.

For the Emrods.

Take the hoofe of a horsfoote, and redd scarlett, burne them
bothe togeather to powder: take white frankensenee. Cast
this powder on a chafingdish of coles and sitt ouer them.

To make a bath for Melancholy:

Take mallowes pellitory of the wall, of each three handfulls
Camomell flowers, Mellelot flowers, of each one handfull,
hollyhocks two handfulls. Isop one greate handfull: fene =
crick seede, of eitseede, of either, one ounce, and boile them
in nine gallons of water, untill they come to three, then
put in a quart of new milke, and go into it bloud warme, or
somthing warmer.

For the faling of the vuila.

Take some leuen and if it be not sowre, temper it with vineger.
lay it to the nape of the neck.

Of Emrodes or Pyles

There are aboute ȳ end of the fundomẽt, fiue veines wᶜʰ are
called Hemoroydale. and are ordeyned of nature to purge the
gross and melancholy bloud in men, as weomens bodies ar pur
ged euery moneth : yf ȳ said purgations come duly yt preserueth
the body from sondry diseases as from ȳ Leper, from Canker
and such like; They be called Hemoroyde of Hema which in
Greeke is blood, and roys, wᶜʰ is flowing : There are diuers kindes
of them for some be like greynes, some are like mulberies, and are
called moralles; and some are smale as Little peces of flesh, about ȳ
fundament and some are painefull, and aposthumẽs. The cause of
these for the most parte, is aboundance of gross and melancholy
bloud, and somtime of flepme, and somtymes of brent choler sent
vnto ȳ sayd place, or els they come thorough the receipt of sharp medy
cines: wherfore by the greate aboundance of such blood, yt chanseth
ȳᵉ the sayd veines swell, and be extended out of the fundament.
bemg very painefull and apostumẽs Therfore if ȳ blud be very
subtile and sharp; and the passion naturall and commg by courses
Then the mouthes of the veines are opened without ȳ melancholy
bloud is purged by the benefitt of nature; and also the sayd matife
bloud watrye and not grosse, then they are like little bladders, or
graines of raysons, and white in colour, soft in touchmg and cause no
greate paine. If they be ingendred of gross flegmatick blud
they are

they are hard like warts or unripe figs, and are not very painfull
except they be ulcered and ioyned with some whott humor //
Their collour is betwene blewnes and rednes, yf they be caused of me
lancholy blood and flegmatick mixt togeather, they are like little
peeces of flesh of black collour: And if they be caused of brent cholerick
blood with melancholy, they are in collo.r & signe, like to a mulbery
and very painefull. There be some, naturall, and some accedentall
The naturall are those which in some budies eucry moneth, or eucry
yere fowre tymes purge gross and melancholy bloud. The acci =
dentall are those which proceed of ȳ forsayd causes, through ill
diett, or other thinges not naturall. wherfore the patient must
avoyde all sharp, salt, and tart thinges that ingender melancholy
blood, as all pulses, the head, the inwards of beasts, and gross
flesh as of kine, Swine, goates, hares, and birds of ȳ riuer: Those
that are ingendred inwardly are naturally, and they are wont to
send out gross blood: And those that were outwardly, send out
watry bloud, somwhat reddish. """"———

_____

See pag.
19, 61.

For the Scyatica.

Take 2.d worth of Cantarides (sow them in a linning-
bagg. stepe them one night in vergiss, & the next morning
apply the bagg to the side of the legg below the knee,
and continue it ther for the space of 6 howers, Then
take it thence & lay to & heplace a cabbage leafe
& when it draws to sume head lett out the blisters

~~Flesh ~~ [struck-through line]

Take planten leaues, and elder flowers, still them wth a quontity
of new milk. When you haue a pottle of that water, take half a
pounde of bitter almonds, blanch them, take your pottle of water
and half an ounce of Mercury boile it on the fier in a pipкin, till
the mercury be consumed; then let it stand till it be colde. and
so putt in yor almonds. ɔmm—

────────────────────────────────────── ɜ₂m—

To make excellent aqua cœlestis. ɔmm—

R͠c. Cinamomi.   ℥ß
Zinziberis   ℥ß
Santhaloram
omniu͡s͡mpulon } ₃ɔ₁
Gariophillorum
Gallangæ   }ana ₃ß
Nucis muscatæ
Macis cubebarū – o   ₃ɟ
Cardamomi veruisₐ
Sem: mpella   }a ₃ɟɟ
zedoria.   ℥ß
S: amsi, sanicul

yt waxeth moist vppon the head, as it wilbe. drye the same one a dish
vppon a Chasindish. and coales. applyng y̌ same. as often as you haue
cause ɔmm—

Par̃ masi ocymi
Rad. Angelicæ
Cariophilatæ
Liquiritiæ
Calami aromati
Phu: scabiosæ
Thmi Calaminth
Palagy serpilli.
Maioranæ Menthæ a ʒ ij
Floru rosaru rub:
Saluiæ Betonicæ
Rosmarinæ
Stæchados
Buglossi Boraginis a ʒ iß
Pul: Corticu Citri ʒ iij
Species Diambreæ
Aromat: Rosat
Diamoschi dulcis

Dia margarito Calide

Elect de gemmis a ʒ iij
Macerant̃ʳ f a · m lib ij Cum optmm claretti siue spirit Cum
vel aquauitæ dieb̕ xv at diſtillent̕, et m aq: inde fluente
Ut diſtillat adde Sonthal odorat, id est Citrmi ʒ ij maschi, abræ
ꝗ gran xv Iulapi rosacæ clarismi lib misce et bene Cooperta, Serua ·······
Bynd the

Binde the ambergreece muske and Saunders, in a cleane
Lymen cloth, and lett ye water as it distilleth dropp through
the muske and amber and ye Saunders, and lett it be tied to
ye pipe of ye Limbeck. Then afterwards add yor Julipp of
Roses into ye water distilled. ....—

_____

This is called ye flower of all oyntments, alias
flos vnguentoru for it is for all maner of
maladies, aches or hurts, new or olde. ....—

vide pag:
30. & 56.

Take Rosen and perrosen, of ech half a pound virgen wax,
olibanum if there be no Olibanum, then somuch frankensence
of eche a qr of a pound, Camfer ij or iij drames of mastick
one ounce of harts sweat a qr of a pound; melt ye that is to be
melted, and pound ye is to be pounded, beaten and fynely searced
and being melted, first put yor tallowe and wax togeather,
then put yor rosen and perrosen togeather to them then your
olibanum then last yor mastick and when all is melted ouer
a soft fier, then strame them thorough a cloth into a pottle of
white wine, Then boile the wine with all the other medicines
togeather, then let it coole till it be blood warme, then put therto
a qr of a pound of Turpentine and be euer stirring vntill yt be
coole, euer beware yor stuff be bloodwarme when you put to your
                                                    Turpentine.
                                                       for

for if it be whott it will marr all yo' stuff / when it is done and
colde inough then anointe yo' hands, with oyle of sweete almonds
and make it vp in roles, and kepe it to yo' vse for the most pretious
salue can be made for all diseases / and for y' goute to spreade
vppon a cloth like a plaister, and put it to y' place greeued, and
yt will not come of vntill y' paine be gon. And if it be for the
goute take half a pound of Lemen mingled w'th y' things aforesayde
w'th y' Campher, you must pound two or three almonds or els y'
Campher will not come to powder // when you make yo' salue in to
roles then you must cass in yo' Campher where y' goute pricks or
akes / Laye to this plaister, and it will drawe out euell humors &
ease you of yo' paine, and this Intreat is good for y' goute, and for
olde sores festred: for manery of all treats it is most clensing, and
a stonrer and will ingender and gather newe flesh, yt is good
for all ould aches, and impostumations of y' body, head, face, or
otherwhere: for sinowes shroonke or shrunke, or to drawe out venim,
stinging or biting of venom'd beasts, to heale all botches, punches
all thinges hardened in the flesh: for noli me tangere to drawe out
all maner aches in y' lymes and head ache, y' splene & y' eies and
breateth all maner of posthumacons or swellings in y' Codds, festers
and Cankers all fluxes of men and weomen: good for Emrods & good to
make any plaister or searcloth, to heale any sore: This Intreat is called
flos vnguentoru, for it cometh of Jesus Christ to a recluse by an Angell
at y' red hill in Almaine, y' w'th wrought many maruells w'th yt, and
neuer had other medicine . »»»—

The order of this medicine ·⸱⸱⸱⸱⸱⸱⸱⸱ —

First cause it to be spred vppon a fayre lynnen clothe plaisterwise
and laye y̆ sume vppon any ioynte wheare the pame is · first
anoynte yŏ ioyntes with oyle of roses · then laye it on · The stuff
of your plaister must be half an inch thick accordinge to the pro =
perly of y̆ same · you must lett it stick and continew ix or x daies
togeather although it putt you to some pame of ache in y̆ mean tyme
yet you must lett it lie on still · for it will bothe drawe out the humors
by little smale pimples and also heale againe, and one plaister must
serue all y̆ tyme of yŏ disease, without any maner of renewing · ⸱⸱⸱⸱⸱ —

To make Oile of Exiter ·⸱⸱⸱⸱ —

Take a pound of y̆ flowers of pagles in May, & stip y̆ in as much
oyle olif as they may easely be layed in, Then take Calamint herb John
Juice of sage ambergreie egremony, sotherwood pennyriall lauender,
speeke pellitory of spaine rosemary, camomill, leaues of sorrell flowers of
Lillies, of each a handfull, gather them in y̆ moneth of June, beate them
in a morter as smale as can be, then take y̆ flowers and wringe them
out of y̆ oile wᵗʰ weary cleane hands, and put y̆ in white wine, a
night and a daie; Then take y̆ herbs with y̆ wine and boile them
togeather with y̆ oile, ouer a soft fier, so long till the wine & water
be wasted

be washed amaye. And thus you shell knowe. take of y̱ liquor
in a spoone, yf the wine and water do appere, then it is not
boiled, but if the wine and water be consumed, then it is well
boyled, Take yt of the fier, and putt it in a stronge bagg of limen
cloth and strayne it betwene two staues, and putt it in a veßell
of tynn or glaß, for no other vessell will hold it; yt will indure
three yeres, and is vvary good for y̱ goute, or where one is brused
and for the palsie, if the patient be anomted therwith, in the
funne in Somer, and by the fier in winter. ,,,,,,,,—

_____

To make Oyle of Swallowes ,,,, — · infra p. 29.

Take twenty Swallowes and put them in a morter, and puts therein
Lauender Cotten, Lauender speike, Camomill snotgmss, ribwort,
balme Vallerian, rosmary tops, woodbine tops, struges of vines,
french mallowes the tops of Ailehouf strawbery strings, tutsen leaues
planten walnut leaues, tops of yong bayes, Isop, violet leaues,
sage of vertue fine romame wormewood. of each of these a handfall
ij of Camomill, ij of red roses, ij ounces of cloues, beaten smale, a
quart of neatsfoot oile, or els asmuch may butter, All these must
be beaten togeather, in a morter, and then put them in an earthen
pott and lett it stand vnder y̱ ground ix daies, and stopp the
pott cleane, and vvary close, then take it vp, and putt in the pott
and.

halfe a pounde of wax, and a pinte of neatsfootoile or els may
butter, and then put the same pott into a pott of water, and
lett it seeth in the same water, with howres, and so take it
out of the water, & frame it & keepe it y whole yere Probatū

To make anointment for y stomak agains
the cost

Take Capons grease y quantity of iij ounces, rosemary m handfulls
and sirop of downeward and stamp it smale, then lett it be putt
into the grease, and lett them boile togeather, untill it be grine,
the stronger it is of the rosemary the better it is, and when it is ready
to be strayned, then putt in half an ounce of y powder of masse
very finely seerced, and then lett it be strained, and use it to y
mouth of the stomak warme.

For y Sciattica

Take a pound of wax, the Juice of margerom red sage, vj spoone
fulls of y iuice of onions troo spone fulls of frankensence nutmegs
cloues mace, and annis seede, of ech a peny worth of turpentine
and applie it uppon leather

For y same
Take Aquabite or Carvinell, y marrow of a deer-shanell or dier-foot
or neats-foot oyle. now putt all theise together in on earthen-pott or
box distill them in y sunne or a pott of warm water. Ms Axholus.

To make a Tisane for y Cough of the Lunges
or for the Cough of the stomak.

Take harts tounge and liuer wort lungworte, Coltsfoote, mayden heare
a little elicompane rootes, raisens of y Sunne skinned, liquoris stamped
omis seede a little brused. Let all these be boyled togeather in fayre
runninge water according to y quantity of the herbs, and when it is
sodden sufficiently strame them all, and so drinke at any tyme
when you will.

To make a powder for the stone to eat with meate
in stead of salt, using yt now and then.

Take the Lunges of a Fox, and wash it in white wine and then laye it
in white wine xij howers, and then drie it in a faire cloth and sett
it into an ouen to be beaten into powder, then take to that a little powder
of liquoris fmely beaten a little annis seede fmely beaten into pouder
and a little suger Candy, beaten into smale pouder; but lett y greatest
quantity of your pouder be of the fox Lunges, and when you eate not
this powder eate two or three tymes a daye, the conserues of redd Roses.

A powder for y Stone.

Take Magisterium Tartari 8 graines Diagrediium 8 grames, mixe
them perfectly together in powder. & this is y greatest proportion
y you must take at one time in a gill of white wine.

A very good almond milk for yᵉ bloudy Flix

Take mutten and boile it in fayre water, and scome it verie cleane
Then putt in a handfull of borage one handfull of prunes, some
whole mace whole Cinamom, the vpper crust of a manchett loafe
boile all these topeather very well vntill the strength of euery thing
be boiled into yᵉ brothe. Then strame it thorough a Cullender,
Then take almonds and pearch them, as you would do peason, and
beale them very fine, skins and all, and putt them into the brothe
and lett them boile againe, ij or iij waumes, then strame it
thorough a faire cloth and season it well with suger, and a little
salte & gene it yᵉ patient to drinke, at any time of the daye.

For one yᵗ is stunge with an Adder

Take mustard seede and bruse it in a woodden dish wᵗʰ dragon
water, then spening the wound with a fine needle, binding the
patient aboue the place where he is hurt, for swelling any further
then bathe the wound all about, as farr as it is swollen wᵗʰ dragon
water, then laye the medicine vppon the wounde, binding it on
with a faire cloth: then yᵉ next tyme you dress it againe anointe
it with oile of roses giuing the patient triacle and dragon water
to drinke when you dress it first.

For a greene wounde

Take rosen, wax and fresh butter, barrowes grease, tryed, of them
a like quantity, boile it untill it leaue boyling, power it uppon
a dish of colde water, then worke it in your hands in little roles
and spread yt on a cloth and laye it on the wounde, and if the
wounde be deepe, then make a tent of lmte, togeather with the
salue and put it into the wound:

A drinke for ye ouerflowing of the Gaule:

Take half a pinte of Goates milk, half a pinte of redd rose water
two ounces of man & xpi half an ounce of white super Candy
three leaues of gould, boile these untill they come to half a pinte
and drinke it morning and euening, fewer tymes

For one that cannot make water.

Take ij or three raddish rootes, scrape them and wash them
veary cleane and slice them into a pinte of white wine, and
boile it from a pinte, to half a pinte, and strame yt, and drinke
yt luke warme.

For the same ·

Take shell snayles, and take out the snayle wash the shell
very cleane, drye them and beate them into powder then take
y̆ powder, & drink it in white wine, or els in thyn broth :.

Another for the same ·

Take black Soape of the st moms you can gett, and worke
yt with white salt very hard, untill it be like paste, and
then role it up like a bale and binde it to your Nauell
with a clothe ·

To help the Vuila ·

Take a peece of fine linen cloth, cut it rounde as bigg as y̆ mould of y̆ head.
laye on it fine flax all ouer not very thick : Then take nigella romana
nutmegs and comen, beate them altogeather to a powder, then laye all y̆
pouder uppon y̆ flax all euer then laye another lane of flax on the same.
as before then take baye salt drie it as drye as yo can, beate y̆ same into smale
pouder and lay it on y̆ flex. all ouer cut a round pece of cloth as the other
before, quilt all these togeather, that y̆ pouder run not abroade. geuing a
speciall marke to y̆ side y̆ salt is on laying this quilt to y̆ mowlde of
y̆ head very whot, the salt side uppermost from y̆ head, and when
　　　　　　　　　　　　　　　　　　　　　　yt

it waxeth moist vppon the head, as it wilbe, drye the same one a dish
vppon a Chafinidish, and ceales applying ẙ same as often as you haue
cause :

An Electuary ẙ Queue Mary was wont to take
for the passion of the hart :

Take damask roses half blowne out cutt of ẙ whites, and beate your
roses very fine, and strame out ẙ iuice, asmuch as you can, you may
putt to it if you will a little rose water, to make it ẙ more moist,
Then take of ẙ finest sugar that you can gett, and make a sirop of it
very thick, Then take rubies and beate them very fine, and likewise
amber and pearle a little amber greece, and mingle all these togeather
with some of the Sirop till it be somwhat thick, then take it morne &
even vppon a knines pointe a little quantity, you may take it els at
any other tyme when you think good : This medicine is very excellent
and so approved :

An aquacomposita for ẙ yellow Jandize

Take iij gallons of very excellent strong ale, ij ounces of Ginger ij ounces
of nutmegos one ounce of Cinamom, one ounce of long pepper one ounce
of graines, one ounce of Galingale, a dram of vnicorns horne iij ounces
of

of annisede and iij ounces of liquoris all these brused, half a pound
of sallandine, half a pound of mercary of the field; asmuch mallowes
All these herbs, finely shred, iij or iiij rootes of fenill, of parslye and
succorye, the piths taten out, shred them also, two ounces of english
saffron finely beaton / y ounces of the grene of goose tords newly
made, y ounces of Elicampana rootes, y ounces of redd wormes, w^{ch}
are comonly called eases; ripp them asunder in y middest, and scrape
out y filth and scoure them in salt, and wash them very cleane
and drie them in a cloth and putt them into the ale; you must
take of the shell snailes, and cut of the heads of them, and slitt them
asunder and scoure them in salt verie cleane, and wash them very
cleane untill all the filth be out Then drye them in a cloth very drie
Take y ounces of these also, and putt all these aforesayd into the ale,
into an earthen pott, one daye and one night, and stir it fiue or (six)
Tymes in that space and then still it either in a lymbeck, of glass, or
of pewter, you must still it in May, and lett the patient drinke it in ale
at morning and euering, one sponefull at a tyme; you may kepe this
in ij or iij yeres, the longer the better : ——— Put also unto these aforesaid
half a pound of reasons of y sun, stonned, and two ounces of hartshorne
finely made into powder ———

For y Green-sicknes.

Take earth wormes open them, wash them clean, drye them in
an Ouen or beat them to powder. giue 2 sponefulls in white
wine in y morneing.

A medicine for the stone

Take an onyon, and cutt out the topp, fill it vp with castle soape and the pewder of franckensence, sett the onion in the whott Jmbers and when it is inough, laye it plaster waye to ye nauell.

A medicine for the Emrods

Take henbane leaues, half a handfull of purslane, as much cromes of bread half a handfull, the yolk of an egg with oile of roses, beate the herbs togeather with the cromes of bread, the yolk of ye egg, and the oile of roses, and make a poultes of them.

For any sore, or pimples in the face

First take bole armmick iiij ounces, camphir one ounce, white copperis iiij ounces put yor camphir and copperis into a stone goddard of earth and seeth them togeather on the fier, and they will become water, and wilbe hard againe; remember to stir them while they be a seething Then beate ye camphir and copperis in a brasen morter very fine and by it self; then beate ye bole armmick by it self, and afterwards beate them altogeather and kepe them close in a bladder, and when any body is hurt, or hath ye skinne broken, Take a pottle of runninge
water

Sett it ouer the fier, till it begin to seeth, then take it of the fier, and
putt iij spoonefulls of the powder into y' same water, and stur them
well togeather and kepe it in a glass, and lett it stand till it be
clere in y' vpper parte, Then washe y' sore with a lynnen cloth
as warme as they can suffer it, and wett a cloth iij or iiij dubble
and laye it vppon the sore, and if it haue a hole in it wet l m te
in y' water, and fill y' whole before you lay on the cloth: and if
any water be left in y' saucer, powre it on y' cloth, that lieth on y'
sore, and bind it well vp: and keepe it very warme, do this
morne and even vntill it be whole. ~~~ You may vse this medicine
after y' oīntment, in the other side wᶜʰ yoᵘ may vse as longe as you liue

For the pimples in the face, if they be neuer so greate

Take one ounce of vnguentū rosatum, of the best you can gett, and half a
pennyworth of y' best brimstone, and a pennyworth of y' best ginger
that you can gett, pare it and beate them bothe very fine, & searce
them, and putt them into yᵉ rosatum: mingle it very well togeather
putt it into a box, Then nointe yoʳ face where it is pimpled xv nights
and in all that tyme you must take hede, that no wett come to yoʳ face:
Then the xvj night, take some oile of sweete almonds, and anointe yᵉ
about one houre before you goe to bedd: and when: (face
                              you:

you are going to bed, take white wine and a little otmeale and wash
your face and it will helpe you and if it were neuer so greate a
sausssyne you must be purged two or three daies before you take it
and be lett blood also if you will / you must keepe a veary good diet.
whilest you take it. ——————

———————————————————————————

An other for the rednes in ye face.

Take ye call and the fatt of the kidneys of a kidd and laye it in red rose
water, a night and a daie. and when you haue so done, mynce it very
smale putt it into some vessell of siluer and keuer it ouer with red
rose water and then keuer the vessell with parchment or paper and
then sett it into a possnet of water and so lett it melt till all ye prease
be consumed and then streme it out Then beate it out in rose water, and
the Juice of lemmons till it comes to a veary pure whitenes. Then
anomte yor face, you may use lamms sewet thus wch is supposed
as good as the other. ——————

———————————————————————————

For ye Rume in ye Eyes, or pain in ye Head.

Take an ounce of Nutmegges, an ounce of Cloues, & an ounce of Mace,
of Rosemary ye worth (i. a good handfull) of sallet oyle a gill. Boyle all
together & lay it on ye crowne of the Head. ye sad ingredients bing dryed &
first beat to powder. ye may lay vnto y^r Eyes Conserue of Roses

———————————————————————————

Balles for the face.

Take greate Allecant reasons, a quarter of a pounde, stone them
but wash them not, and beate them in a morter very fine take as many
almonds, not Jordans but of y comon sort and blanch them, and drye
them in a cloth very well, and beate them in a stone morter also very
fine when you haue done thus, to them bothe mingle them bothe together
and beate to'm againe and putt to it half a quarter of a pounde of browne
leauened bread wheaten bread : and beate them altogeather and mingle
them well togeather, and then take it and make it in little balles and then
wash is y face at night with one of them in fayre water. Yf you will
haue this only to wash yo hands, put in a little Venice soape, but putt
none of that in for youre face.

Oile of
swallowes.
fo. 18.

A singuler Ointm: for any Ache or Bruise.

Take Rosemary-toppes, Lauender-cotten, Tyme, y strings
of strawberries, french-Mallowes & southernwood, y toppes of
Bayes, dill, Asowe ana 2 handfulls. Take 30 swallowes out
of y nest young & flush, & pound them very small in a stone
morter till y see noe subtance but feathers. Then pound all y
Herbes wth y swallowes & an ounce of Cloues therto, & in y pounding
putt to it by little & little 2 pound of Barrowes greafe; then putt
it all into a pott & couer it close, & lit it boile for y space of
2 houres, putting to it at y first before yu boile it a Quart of
Neats-foot oile. Then take it off & strain it, & couer it close
& let it stand 10 or 12 daies; & then boil it again an houre
& yf need bee put to it a pound of Barrowes greafe more.
Then strain it & putt it up, & keep it for youre use.

A deume Plaster for any ache (which
being laied to y⁰ place greeved, taketh awaye
the paine so soone as it is once throughly warme

Take two pound of Enwrought wax, of deere suett half a pound, of perrosen
fower pound, of cloues and mace, of each two ounces, half an ounce of
saffron, of rosen two pound of black pitch a q̃ of a pound: melt that is
to be melted, and powder and searce that is to be powdred Mingle all
togeather Uppon a soft fier except y⁰ cloues maces and saffron Then
take a pottle of redd wine and by little and little powre it to y⁰ salue, stirring
it togeather, and when it is melted, straine it into a cleane pann, and then
put in y⁰ powder of cloues, maces and saffron, casting it abroad Uppon y⁰
ingredientes, and stir it well togeather a good while, and let it stand till it
be somwhat cold and then anoint well y⁰ handes with oile or soft greace
and while it is somwhat warme, make it Up in bigg roles and driue it
with y⁰ hands often tymes, and then it wilbe coullered like wax, and so
make it Up in good roles.

For numnes of members.

Take and anointe the greese if it cometh of colde with oile of Woodbine
and if it cometh of heat. Use Populion.

For the falling sicknes

Take the seedes of Satteren and drinke 3 of them in fine powder
morne and even for fourty daies, yt remedieth.

For the dymnes of the eies

Take of the water that is stilled of strawberries, and wash ȳ eies
with yt; Likewise it doth quench ȳ heate of the face, and take
awaye the redd spotts of ȳ same, if you vse it xiy daies togeather.

To stopp the Flux

Take the Raspes berries, and boile them in red wine, and drinke
of it often times warme, there is none like to this, and it quencheth
s̄t antonies euell, as diascoridis reporteth lib: 4 chap: 34

To heale the Emrods

Take Aaron called Cuckow pintle, and boile it in oile-Olife and
warme applie it twise in the daye, it healeth it wᵗʰ in ix daies at
the furthest

For sore eies a remedy most excellent

Take rose water, womans milke and the white of an egg, beate them togeather, and putt of it into the eies, yt taketh away the dymnes burning, rednes and swelling and cleareth the sight

---

To heale a fellon or Bile

Take beane meale and fenecrick in pouder ana ʒ ij mix it with hony a sufficient quantity, and applie of it to the greese morne and even, yt helpeth

---

To heale y greate heate in y brests of women or in y privy members of men

Take the iuice of hemlock and applie it to the greef 2 or 3 tymes in y daye ana wett a cloth in it and laye it to the greef use it 3 or 4 daies, yt quencheth St Antonies fier

---

For a sore Breast. or y Wolf.

℞ Pitch or Rosin ℥iij. Bee-wax ℥iij. Sheep-suitt ℥iij. all boyled together takeing away y feume. then take a piece of new-linnen cloath vnwashed fro y weauer or steep it in it of both sides like a fear-cloath, or cutt it in pieces according to y wound, or yf it need a tent take some of y faid plaister & make a little tent or put it in. the lay on y plaister & yf it doth not curdle make y pultice of swea-milk or otmeal, but in noe case let y wounds shutt of themselues, for they will breik in another place. when it is cured anoint it wth y oyle of swallows or some other oyle to take away y rednes out of y breast. y party when she is cured must keep her breast rolt for half a year after.

To cleere a dymme sight of the eies

Take the Juice of Selendine and put it into a brasen vessell
with the like quantity of hony being clarified and boile them
to thicknes, use to put of it into ye eies morne & euen it cleereth y^{em} w^{ll}

For the Jaundize and Choller

Take ʒij of the rootes of Sollodiu annis seede in powder ʒj boile
them in a quart of white wine, till half be wasted, then strame
it and drinke of it morne and euen ʒj at a time, not to drinke
after it two howres, use it ix daies.

For ache, stitch, or swelling. r

Take half a peck of earth wormes and putt them into haye to
skowre themselues shifting them 3 times in 24 howres wth new
haye, then stamp them smale in a morter and putto them a pottle
of malmsey and a pottle of muskaden, then boile them till more then
half be wasted then strome it and kepe it for yor use to anoint
the greef wth morne and even.

For the Windecclick or the Stone

Take a quart of muskadill or malmsey and seeth in it two heads of
garlick being peeld and brused and the rinde of a lemmon or the
iuice of one, seething them till half be wasted, then straine it and
drinck of it morne and euen warme, 8 or 9 spoonefules at a tyme

---

To take cornes from the feete also to drawe prick, neale or arrowhead from the flesh

pag: 38.

Take wax ℈j rosne ℈j ʒi and of the powder of Aristolochia rotunda
and of longa of each ʒij melt the wax and the resin then putte yor
powder finely beate and searst and stur it till it be colde, and laie of it
to anie of the greeues morne and even plaster wise yt remedieth in short
space, as it hath bene tried. 9·

To drawe the rewme from the gummes

Take of the roote of pellitorie of spaine ʒj beeng in fine powder then
infuse in it stronge vineger, and make rounde smale peles with it,
and holde one now and then in thy mouth, this will purge yr gommes
and ease the toothe ache

To cleanse the face from spotts blanes from
shingles blisters and pimples ﹒﹏﹏

Take the roote of Briony ʒj made into fine powder and putto it ʒj of
the powder of femerick mix them (wth oile of Tartora in the forme of
an ointement and anointe the greef with it; or take the roote and
seethe it in a quart of white wine to a pinte, then straine it, and put
to it camphire ʒj and wash the face euery night, wth a sponge wett in
it and let it drye in, and it remedieth the greefe ﹒﹏﹏

━━━━━━━━━━━━━━━━━━━━━━━━━━

For the Migrome ⁜

Take of the galle of an Ox, and mix it wth sanguis dragonis the
weight of an egg, and the powder of a nutmeg, spread of this in the
inner pell of the ox galle and laye it to the fore part of the head as a
plaister and lett it lie till it falle of alone, dreſſing it three times, yt
cureth the greefe certainly ﹒﹏﹏

━━━━━━━━━━━━━━━━━━━━━━━━━━

For the Coughe ﹒﹏﹏

Take a pinte of clarett wine hony ʒ ꝫ annis seede in fine powder
ʒ viij boile these to the forme of an electuary and vse it morne
and even ʒj at a time ﹒﹏﹏

━━━━━━━━━━━━━━━━━━━━━━━━━━

(For shortnes of the breath

Take clarified hony a pinte, and putto it the powder of Erringe
rootes ʒ vi, fenell seede ʒ .y, cloues, nuttmegos, ginger, longe
pepper black pepper and mace ana ʒ .y, clarret wine halfe a
pinte boile them a while on the fier, and keepe it for yo vse
eate of it morne and euen ʒ .y at a time, you may giue it to any
(woman wth childe at any tyme .

(A medicine for pissing a bedd

Take of the powder of harts horne, ana take morne and euen ʒ .j
for 12 daies in yo drinke, refrayning from butter fatt meate and
oyle and pottage for the tyme .

For ye heate of ye body of what cause soeuer it be.

Take endif water halfe a pinte, of milke a pinte, brewe them well togeather
then seethe them and when they seeth, putt into yt iij spoonefulls of ginger
and it will curde, take awaie the curde cleane, and drinke of it morne
and euen 7 or 8 spoonefulls, bloud warme .

To stopp a flux

Take Rice ʒ iiij seeth it in faire water a quart, till it breake, take that liquor and putto it Sinamom in fine powder good store, and drinke of it two or three times, as yo listt in y daye in me warme

For the Tisick

Take horehounde wormewood Isop and calammt ana aʒ bruse them and putt them into ij gallons of stronge ale or beere for 24 houres, then strame it and to every quarte putt ʒ ij of suger in fine pouder, and eate man? xpus and pennedice morne and even ʒ ij at a time, not for to drinke after it for ij houres Ose it 24 daies

For a Stiche or Pluresy

Take a Costard apple, cutt of the topp and take out the coare, then putt into the hole ʒ j of the powder of Olibanum, and laie on the topp againe and sett it againt the fier to roast, and giue to the greeued of it, ij or iij times in the daie to eate

For burninge or skalding.

Take graye sope and anointe the greese wth it 4 co^wres togeather, that you lett it not be w^thout noint~ing half a q^r of an howre for those 4 houres this will saue it from blist~ring, and heale it in 48 houres.

To take awaye Cornes

Take an Iron and make it whott and seare the corne with it then laie to it a platter of Galbanu and turpentine mixt togeather, and it Will take it out and heale it in 9 daies.

To take awaie the rednes of the face.

Take quilted grisse z^j and putto it pouder of brimstone fineły grounde z^j and xx cloues in fine powder, mix these well togeather and anointe the face every nighte when yo^u goe to bedd and in ye morninge, wipe yor face with a peece of fine cotten white, and wipe net twice in one place, and it will heale it in xv daies, you may eate no broathes nor drinck anie wine in that time.

To heale a greene Wounde.

Take Vennice Turpentine ʒij mix yt with as much suger, and
applie it to the Wounde.

For the botche.

Take honie and the yeulk of an egg, and mix them with brunt allome
and laie it on linte, and laye it too: and a plaister of grene treate uppon
yt, and it will heale it.

For such as do vomitt and cast up theire meate.

Take oile of spike, and anointe the stomake with it, then take a fine cloth,
wett it in water and doble wringe it being two folde, laie it to ye stomack
colde uppon the oile, use it vj or vij daies, it will remedy thee.

For the skurff and scab in the face.

Take mallowes good store, and seeth them in urme well, and wash
the skurff with it.

For such as haue the Lunacy.

Take the iuice of Perselle and mix it with ǵinger and putt of
it into ý nose with a Seringe 2 or 3 times in the daye being
bloud warme and it will remedy ý same in 3 or 4 daies.

For the yellow Gaundize

Take linar worte and stamp it and take ʒ iij of the Juice and hony
ʒ iij being clarified boile them togeather in the forme of a sirop and
Use it 5 or 6 times in the daye ʒ ij at a tyme.

To clense the Vrine and reynes.

Take the rootes of mallowes ʒ ij seethe them in a quart of White wine
till halfe be wasted then strame it and drinck it morne and euen
it clenseth grauell. it is good for the Siattica, rupture or bluddy flux.

To stint the bloud of the Piles

Take ý iuice of yarrowe and drinck it this is proued, and laye ý pouder
of burnt garlick therto, for it is good for them

For a benommed member. ~~~~

Take the leaues of white willowe and seeth them in faire water, and
when they be well sod, then take a quart of vineger and mix the leaues
therewith and make a plaister of them; and lay it to ye benommed member
and it will make hym whole in five or vj daies ~~~~

For deafnes ~~~~

Take the galle of a Hare and mix it with womans milk, and putt of
it into the eare warme, and stopp it close wt black woll, and it healet
in nyne daies. ~~~~

For ache of the back or iointes ~~~~ th olde

Take ij spoonefulls of ye iuice of bettony, and mix it with a sponefull of honny
and putt therto x pepper cornes in pouder and mix it wth wine or ale, and
drinke it many times, and it will make them well. ~~~~

For ache or swelling in any iointe

Take hemlocke, sheeps tallowe, and oile olife, frye them togeather and
laie it to as a plaister ~~~~

To stint bloud in a wounde ·

Take broome and shaue of the vpper pill of it and take the pill next
the wood and make splagetis of it and laie them to the wound it
will staunch the bloude ·

To drawe out wood iron or bone out of a wound's

Take woodbin leaues and stamp them smale and laie them to a wound,
and it will drawe them out you must take violett leaues and stamp
them and strame them with stale ale and drinke it daily for ⁵ or ⁶
daies morne and euen ·

For a wound yᵗ hath perill in it ·

Giue yᵉ sick to drinck at yᵉ begininge pigrll bagell and sanacle hearb robar
de maisellon epremony daisyes avayebrode sentory untorosi cresses tanze
malloroes and hemp of each alike, mitch mather half asmuch as of all the
rest of yᵉ hearbs stamp them well then strame it and lett it soie then
giue the wounded to drinck and if he casts it it is a signe of life, then
search yᵉ wound diligently and dress it vp ·/ this drinke is good for the
fister canker and many other thinges you must giue it daily to the
wounded man fasting ⁵ or 6 sponefulls at a tyme ·

A drinke to heale a wounde or sore

Take yarrowe, bugle, avene, sweete brier, topps and sanickell, of coche alike stamp them smale, and straine them with white wine, and giue yt to drinck morne and even as neede requires.

A soveraine water.

Take sentory and stamp it smale and put it to cleare ale and stale, then lett it stand 24 houres, then still it and take that water and putte it ginger in pouder, annis seede, fennell seede, and parceley seeds āna ʒij ginger but ʒij, these are to a pottle of the water, lett them stand 24 houres then still them againe and vse this water morne and even for a principall medicine for y coughe, ache of y sides impostumes of the body, or anie euell in y brest, or greeues of the spirituall members yt causeth a man to haue on appetite to his meate, that cannot eate.

To take away spotts in the face.

Take the rootes of wilde vepper and mallowes of each alike seeth them well and braye them well with ysell and oile olif hony and wine, and therewith anointe y skurs or spotts of y face, it remedieth.

For the dropsey a good medicine

Take of the flower deluce rootes made as cleane as may be then stamp
them very smale and straine them strongly into a pewter dish, and
leit it rest that the groundes may settle then take the clere water
and putt it into a glass, and putto it While stone suger and giue the
sick one sponefull, if he be vncoked to cast, take a sponge, welt it in
vineger and hold it to y beck of y throte, it staieth y same Probatum

---

For the Reynes that be sore

Take tanzey a good quantitie stamp it well with sheeps tallow and
frie them well togeather, and warme laie it to y back vse it 4 or 5 daies

---

For serenes of the back wth bruse or stroke

Take Epremeny, smaledg and mouse eare stamp them smale, and putt
thereto bacon prease and Isell and fry them, and make a plaister, and
lay it warme to y back

For one that spitts bloud

Take nepp and stamp it smale, and take the suice, and drinck it and you
shall cast out the bloude

A Powder for the Fister

Take Arromit and salt and burne them to powder then take Vergreace
pepper and White glass and mustard seede make them into fine powder
of each alike then mix them and laie of them to y sore as often as neede
requireth, yt will heale perfectlie

For one that is Wounded

Giue hym the Iuuce of parceley to drinck and it shall never ranckle
nor fester, on Warrant

To know Whether a sick man shall liue or die
certenly proued manie tymes

Take a penny weight of land cressede and giue y sick to eate three
daies togeather, fasting, and to drinke a draftt of Water after it or Wine
if he cast it vp he shall die y or els take tormentell hayberries and mirre
ana ʒj make these into fine powder, mix them well togeather giue y sick
of it to drinck, in stale ale ʒj at atyme if he cast it vpp he dieth of the
the same sicknes, if he retene yt he shall liue, the bayes purge, the
tormentall voideth all venome and rawe meates lyinge in the stomak
and y mirre suffreth no corruption in the body of man

For y same purpose.
Take a little of their Water & putt into Milk. & yf they dye a dogg
will not eat it. & yf they liue a dogge will eat it.   &c: N.C.

For the Quartane fever

Take triacle, wax, oile olye, and barrowes greace ana ℥ j melt the wax
in the oile, and putt it whott into a morter with the rest, and worke
them well togeather to an ointment, and anointe therewith both the
stomak and back against the fier, and wrapp the body vpp in a fine
sheete well warmed and laie hym in his bedd and couer hym well
that he may sweate, thus dress hym three tymes and be whole

To take away freckels in the face

Take the snailes with the shell and stampe them smale and temper them
with the white of an egg and rubb the face with it morne and even
vse it daily it will help:

For a saseplene face

Take a white lilly roote and swines greace, and brimstone, but first putt
the brimstone in whot water a while, then stampe them well togeather
and grinde them fine with a little franckenfence, and vse it y quick siluer
litarge of gould brimstone boras and oile of Tartar is good for saseplene faces
garlick, onions, leekes and redd wine, they maintein y saseplen face

For all maner of Agewes.

Take rewe wormewood, and sotherne wood, and seeth them in wine
and drinck thereof three daies before the fitt cometh, and come nere
no fier, nor eseame furious meates.

To heale a wounde.

Take Sentory and make powder of it, and strowe of it on the wounde
it will heale the same

To heale a wounde lightlie.

Take mather tanzey hemp cropps, the cropps of redd colle, the crops of redd
nettles and y cropps of redd briars asmuch of y one as of the other saue of
the mather half asmuch as all y rest stamp them smale each by them selues
then mix them togeather and make balles of it asmuch as greate beanes
then drye them in an oven, and when they be drie putt them into some box
to keepe untill you haue neede of them: The vertue of them is to heale
anie wounde: to take two of them and beate them, and putt the same into
wine or stale ale and drinck it fasting in y morne, and to walke a good while
after use them as neede requires.

To cleere a wounde ———

Take the powder of harts horne, and it will take awaie all euell
humors being strewed vppon the wounde and drie it vpp soone //

———————————————————

For a sore y is open and will not close vpp.

Take Incense and arromint of equall partes and grinde them together into fine pouder and laye it to y sore morne and even ——

———————————————————

A pretious water for sores olde or newe

Take canouse that leather neuer came in, a rottle of the best worte
a gallon of lee made of wood asshes togeather then take roche allonne
and of the croppes of mather ana iij ʒ, boile them togeather a little
and putt it into an earthen pott and couer it close and lett it stand
till you haue neede thereof it heales all maner of sores olde or newe

———————————————————

To staie the flux ——

Take a quart of faire Water and boile it in perrewincles a handfull
s mamom iij in fine pouder a lemmon cutt in peices boile them till
half be wasted then straine it and sweete it with suger drink it morne
and even. ——

———————————————————

A Water for diuers sores well tried

The vrine of yong children knauish and wanton, a pottle of the
clerest vineger that may be goden and take stronge wine vineger a
quart, putt them togeather and putte them, wood asshes and vnslackt
lyme of each a pretty quantity and seeth it till y third parte be wasted
then lett it stand till it be cleere, then putte it salt armonike, salt geme,
salt nitar and allum de plumbe ana ʒ ij made into pouder and stopp
the glasse close and keepe it for yo vse this water will kill in fower
daies any naturall cancker fester dead flesh and wenns yt kills
the webb in y eie if you touche it with y water but once it is good for
many other thinges more as it hath bene prooued

To staie the Flux

Take wheat flower putt it into a bagg and tye it hard togeather then seeth it
for 24 howres in faire water and it wille veary hard, then lett it coole
and scrape of it into milk & lett y suk drinck of it morne and even

For swellinges

Take turnip rootes and boyle vnto a pumies and laie of it
warme to the swellinge morne and even.

For the toothe ache

Take the inner pell of the ashen plant and burne it to ashes
by it self then moist of the asshes and make a body of it and
laye of it behinde ẏ eare as a plaister, it remedieth ẏ same ⁘

For the bitinge of ẏ brest and stomak

Take pepper ℥ß in fine powder, baye berries ʒij likewise in powder
mix them well togeather and drink ʒß of it in luke warme wine
it ceaseth the torments of the body ẏ bitinge of ẏ brest and stomak ⁘

A Souereigne Water for Sores.

Take salundine, rewoorte and yarrowe, of each two good handfulls
boile them in a gallon of water to a pottle, then straine it and putto
it aqua fortis ʒj quick siluer ʒj and lett them stand it wilbe
like mercury sublime; This water will heale all sores & fistelos
as it hath bene often proued ⁘

A certaine remedy for ẏ toothach
if it proceedes from heate
Take 2 or 3 plantan leaves cutt them smalle with
a knife & putt them in a little peice of linn=
inge clothe & streine 2 dropes of ẏ iuce
into ẏ parties contrary eare & before you
can tell to 20 ẏ cure is done.

Henry Cholmeley

For the running out of ỹ fundament

When it is out wipe it cleane then putt into it six or seven grames of baye salt and putt it in a warme clothe use it 2 or 3 times it helpeth

---

To stopp ỹ flux or gomora passhio / Gonorrhæa.

Take comfori knotgrass bursapastoris and plantine of each a handfull the knuckles of x or xij legges of mutton seeth them well in a gallon of water till it come to ỹ pintes then straine it with salt and eate of it or drinck of it warme morne and even x or xij sponefulls when it is colde it will be like a Jelley

---

For the Epileptia Infallible (ỹ Falling-sicknes it remedieth in six daies.

Take the after burden of a woman and drie it in a pott till you make powaer of it and give of it to the diseased for vj daies fasting in the mornig ỹ ß at a tyme in ale or bere not to drinke after it for two houres you must use the burden of the male childe to the woman and the femmine to the man / This is prooued boise of man woman and childe Infallible

---

For ỹ same. ỹ falling-sicknes.

Take ỹ hearts of Moules dryed into powder. or drinck Cowslip-wine

ỹ fame

Take a pottle of old Ale w̄out hops: halfe an ounce of Nutmeg: a q̄ter of an ounce of Ginger. half a q̄ter of an ounce of Cynamon; & half a q̄ter of a pound of Sugar beat ỹ spices together in a morter put them in ỹ Ale & take a q̄ter of a pound of Piony-root, & bruise it in a morter & put it into ỹ Ale w̄th ỹ spices, & let it stand 3 nights. & then drinck a draught of it 9 morninges together stir it well when ỹ drinck it & yf it cure not w̄th ỹ first 9 morninges. rest fro it 2 or 3 dayes & then use it agayn & so may for a Rheume. And every night when he goes to bed apply to his forehead Rosemary bruised & a Nutmeg grated, & white wine viniger lukewarme & so for red

For greate bodies as y tympany or dropsey in y legs

Take white wine three gallons, stronge beere iij gallons, safeperella Sene liquoris skrapt ana j β cortex ligna j t browsed coliqumtida, safsafrage ana ʒ d. boile them clos in balneo maria 24 howres, then lett it coole, then lett it runn thorough an Jpocras bagg, and ad to it ℥ β of mithridatum give it morne noone and at night at each tyme ʒ iij. Use it as neede requires, it is good for most diseases

For the stone in the reynes and bladder

Take ramsyns and y leaves of lond Willowes stamp them smale and wrimpe out the iuice and putto it a little longe pepper and lett y diseased drinke of it in stale ale, yt will ease hym incontmently. y

A most pretious water to recover one at y ponite of death

Take y spirit of wine rectified iiij tymes oile of sulphur and of vitriall ana ℥ β Julip of violatts ℥ 60 mix them togeather in a glasse and give to the sick of it ʒ j at a tyme, it recovereth them that lye at y pointe of death it mittiga teth all paines and dissoluith all infirmties it breaketh all colerick humors preserveth y stomack it causeth appetite it helpeth all kinde of fevers and preserveth both man and woman in good state, vsing it somtymes

A Dyett drincke.   53.

Take of pollepodū the weight of ——— ʒij
of Spicnard the weight of ——— ʒij
of Junctus Odoratus the weight of ——— ʒij
of mergerō the weight of ——— ʒij
of Seltwell the weight of ——— ʒij
of Rubarb the weight of —— j dram.
of Sinamō beaten the weight of ——— ij ℔
of Senay bruised the weight of ——— iiij ℔
of Galingall, the weight of ——— ʒij

    Beat all this a sunder then mingell
then to gether then put them in a fine limin
bagg, to tow gallons of strong ayle and putt
it into a earthen stone pott, put a small
sticke in to the bagg of the lenth of the vese
to keep the bagg a littell shorte of the bottam
tie the bagg close to the sticke all the tuppe
when yo ayle is a day olde drink a good
draught warme in the morning fasting
and last att night and att yo mayles
cowloe. do this till yo fen yo body truely
skourede :

54.

Right noble knight your kindnis and loue
hath bene alwayes suck as makes me be(us)
presumptius of more fauores which if it pleaso
you now to grant I will not in that mattere be
euer so troublesom to you againe it is for thoso
as so I desire to be thankfull to for manye curtisi
receaued at thor hands, my sute is for a stagg
which if it pleaso you to grant me I shall
thinke you doe me as great a pleasure at
this tyme as I can desire of you, I
beseech you sir for all thor fauores yt euer you
haue done me deny me not in this and
if you do grant it me let me haue it while
speed for I to packe it and send it up
to london befor yt first of august, though
harye Chamley be not heare I must not
forget to present his seruice and thanks
for all your curtisses thus with my seruice
presented to you desyring god to grant
you what you can best wish for your soule
health and worldly former I will athwayes
rest your assured and thankfull frend

tha[n]kes for

margrett

60

A medicine to cure by the weapon published
amongst other things by Rodolphus Goclenius
Professor of Phisicke in wittenberghe in
the yeare 1608. Intituled the magneticall
cure of a wound. Pag: 261 —

Take of the mosse of the skull of a strangled man
2 ounces, of the mumia of mans blood, ½ ounce and
a halfe, of earth wormes washed in water, or wine and
dryed, one ounce and a halfe, of Hæmetitis 2 ounces
of the fatt of a Boare, bore pigge, and Bore of each
2 drams, of oyle of Turpintine two drams, pound them
and keepe them in a longe narrow pott, make this
when the sunne is in Libra, dippe into the oyntment
the yron or wood, or some sallow sticke made wett with
blood in opening the wound. Lett the patient washe
his wound in the morninge with his owne vrine
or cleare water, and bynde it with a cleane cloth,
alwaios wyping away the matter.

a glister

take posset drinke made of small ale, annisseed
fennell seede, browne sugar, candie & hunny.

for paines in the heade

take bay salte, rosemary seede, and fennell
of our ... one ... one handfull beate
them well togither & boyle them in a pint
of vinigar & a pint of rose water and til
they be ... like a plaster   for Headache.
R. of oile of Roses Vineger & juice of Rew are alike quantity.
mingle them together & anoint ye head often times therwith.   or:
R. ye braines of a Crow, seeth it & eat it. or it will help.
                                                      H. Cro.

61

vide pag 30.1

A Salve to cure all maner of Sores both old & newe.
alsoe it cures Impostemes & Inflamations.

Take Rossen & prossen of each a pound. Virgines Wax & Franc=
kinsence of each a quarter of a pound. Mastick an ounce. Harts tallow
or deer-suitt a quarter of a pound. Camphire 2 drames. Malt those y^t
are to be melted, & pounce those y^t are to be pounced fine & cover th
& boyle th^5 over a fyre. then strein them through a clean canvass
clothe in a pottle of White wine, then boyle ye Wine & all together
then lett it cool till it be noe warmer then blood. Then put to it
a quarter of an ounce of Turpentine, evermore stirring it till it
be through cold. But beware y^t ye stuff be noe warmer then blood
when y^u put in ye Turpentine. Then when it is cold make it up
in Rolles, & keep it for ye most best Salue y^t is to be used.

To help ye Spleen wth great speed.

Let blood under ye toung in one of those 2 veines y^t is on that side where
ye milt lyeth, that being done take mustard & mixe it wth ye vrine of
a Boy, & lay it between 2 cloathes, & lay it on ye sore place one night. &
then y^f it be not well y^f it still vntill it be helpt. Leonardo Phiorovanti

A plaister for Wormes.

Take of Camomil, Fetherfewe, Wormewood, Tansey. Herbe-grace; ye blades
of vnsett Leekes & Parsley of each half a handfull. Fry them in fresh
butter, & putt them into a linnen bagge & apply them above ye regiment of
ye stomack as hott as ye patient can suffer.

A mollifying Glister.

Take of Cowes-milke a pinte, ye yolkes of 3 Egges. 3 ounces of Honney.
2 ounces of Oile-olive: make all this into a Glister & give A Worme.

To stopp Blood.

Take linnen-clothes & dipp them in ye green some where Frogges have their
spawne 3 dayes before ye new-Moon.

To pull out a toothe.

Take Wormes when they be a gathering together dry them vpon a hott tyle stone.
then make powder of them, & what toothe y^u touch wth it will fall out. H. C.
Or ye wheat-flower & mixe it wth ye milk of Spurge & therof make a paste or dowe
wth ye wth fill ye hollow of ye tooth & leave it in a certein time & ye tooth will fall out.

Take of y[e] flowers of Pomgranats, and frankincence, each
a dragm[e] and a half, which maye be about the wayte
of xij[d]. the best bole armoniacke one ounce, and of
the best aloes half an ounce, of choyse mastickes
and dragons blood each one dragme. White wax,
oyle of roses, and venice Turpintine, as much of
each, as will serue to make it a plaster.

Quene Elisabeth her powder for wind,

take ginger, Cinamon, Gallingall, of each one ounce
Anise seeds, Caroway seeds, fenell seeds of each one half an
ounce; mace, nutmegs of each tow drames, of
setwall one drame, ponde all together, [or searce them,] & putt
therin one pound of white suger. vse this powder
after or before meate at anie time. [it expells wind] it comfor
teth y[e] stomack, & helpeth digestion. /

Scurvigrass-Drinck. / A Dyett,
to be taken 2 houres before meales.

—Take Zarsaparilla ℥6. Polipod of oake ℥4. Sene ℥4.
Annice Fennall & Caroway-seeds, ana ℥i. Liquorize scraped &
bruised ℥2. Agrimony & Maidenhaire ana 2 handfulls. Liuer=
wort one handfull. Scurvigrass 2 peckes. new Beer or Ale
3 gallons.

Dr Butler's receipt. / out of this and former. page

alias. Take Polypode, Spiknard, Squinant, forked-Ginger, Margerum, Galingal,
Serrwell ana 6 penny weight. Annice-seeds, Saffafrass & Plantain ana
y weight, Sceny y leaues of eddy as much as all y rest. y aforesaid
particulers being grosly beaton into powder, half a peck of Scurvigrass
stamped, put all y Scurvigrass & y drugges into a bagge, & hang it with
a pack thred in 2 gallons of strong Ale, & stop it so close as noe
ayre may come to it to dead y Ale, or else covering Ale every 4th day
with fresh barme or Yeast— & drinck thereof 9 or 10 dayes.

this drinck. It purgeth all Humors in y body. It will not suffer
y Bloud to putrify: neither fleame to haue dominion: nor Melancholy to
haue exaltation. It doth multiply bloud. It helpeth all will in y body.
It purgeth Rewme. It defendeth y stomack. It nourisheth, preserveth
& preserveth Youth. It engendreth good collour. It comforteth y sight. It
nourisheth y minde. & is good against y Stone.

My La: Fleetwood's
receipt. by Mrs Dimmoc

Green Oyntment made in may
infused Sage rue wormwood. Camomile Chickweed
Elder Tops: mallows of Each one hand full
shred ym Small—put to ym half pd of may but
unwashed or Salted—put to it half p of Shuet
2 oz. of oyl Spike & 2 oz: oyl olive let ym boyl
Gently on a soft fire till the but: & Suet
be well melted yn Strain it and Keep for Use
very good for bruises & Strains

how to make the greene oyntment

Take of red sage & rewe of ech a pound, or a quart. & of yong
bay leaues & wormwood of ech li: picke tham well, butt
wash tham not, shread tham smale: & beat tham well in a
morter: then take 3li of sheeps suitt hot fro the sheeps bely
sread it smale & beat itt with theese hearbes vntill itt be all
of a culler: then putt tham all in a faire boule wth a pottle of
the best oyle oliue & worke itt all together vntill itt bee
alyke soft: & then putt itt into an earthen pott, stop it
close for eight days space: then take itt & boyle itt in a
faire pane wth a soft fyer & when itt is halfe boyled putt
to itt 4 ounces of oyle of spike then boyle tham all well
together vntill it come to a perfect greene, ~~butt take~~
~~heed that yo boyle itt~~ & then strane it throwk a faire
linen cloth into a galley pott, or some other pott, covering
it close, butt take heed that yo boyle it softly vntill
it come to the culour, & thus its made,

the vertue of this oyntment

If yo anoynt the stomacke wth it, it helpeth ye digestion
& expelleth all obstruckions; rubb it on the small of the
backe, & it helpeth the stone: the quantitye of half a
bea well rubd in behynd the eare, being stoped with

blacke wooll helpeth all paines therin, it is allso good
against all aches & Fellons & swellings of wounds,
& allso against tooth ache proseeding of cold rume it
helpeth anye bruse or straine in vaine or sinnow
tis good for the cramp & ~~sight~~ sciatica & all
manner of burnings & scaldings strickes or stiffe
or straines in man or Beast

it is made only in maye,

For a Consumption.

℞ 2 Gallons of ye strongest wort made of Ale. Boyle
it & scume it very clean soe long as it will beare a scume.
Let it boyl gently a whole day or longer till it come onto ye
thicknefs of an Electuary. Soe eat of it wth a Liquorize stick
morning & evening, & as often of a day as you can. Probatum

A Jelly for ye same.

Take a Red Digge neither too fatt nor too lean, drefs it
clean & boyle it in a sufficient quantity of water wth Maidenhaire
& Coltfoot of either an handfull, Liquorize scraped &
bruisd j ounce. Reisons of ye sunne stoned, & Curranee of either
a handfull. 6 Dates sliced, & 6 chiues of large Mace, & lett them
boyle to ye height of a Jelly. then straine it & putt to it as much
Sugar as will make it sweet, then putt to it j Nuttmeg sliced
Cynamon 2 drames, ginger j drame, & 6 or 8 spoonfulls of
Red-rose water. Clarify it wth ye white of an Egge; & runne it
through a Jelly bagge & referve it for your vse. And
of this ye are to take a good draught warme, first & last.
Dr Butler.

For the Sciatica.

Take ye Gall of a Bull or Oxe, let ye moisture therof
into some little Skellet & set it over a soft fyre &
a little scume will arise, wch must be taken off, putt
therto as much of ye best Aquavitee as ye clear of ye gall
wch remaineth is, & haue before hand halfe an ounce of
Pepper (as small beaten as possibly may be) ready & putt
therto also, & as much of ye Marrowe of a Horse-shanke
as a good Wallnutt, or for want therof an ounce of ye
Oile of Camomill. & When they haue been a little over
ye fire incorporated togeather, take it off, & keep it close
covered or stopped in some Bottle or Pott of stone or glass
till you vse it.   The Vse.
When yu will vse it, yu must shake it well togeather and
putt forth very near ye quantity of 2 spoonefulls thereof
into a sawcer, & while it is warmeing on a few coales or
before ye fyer, warme a course-linen clothe ye is made
soft wth wearing as hotte as can be suffered & lett ye party
kneel setting ye grieved place towards ye fire to warme &
wth that clothe soe made hotte chafe ye place a good space
togeather, And after it is soe chafed lett one wth ye fingers
doe on that in ye sawcer as hott as it can be suffered, &
when it is all done on, stroake ye place downeward, & for
ye quantity is vsed, aime at soe much for another time as
goeth in most of it.   And vse this, 2 warming & Morning
15 daies togeather.   Probatis. by mr Hunt of DDRS.

For ye Splen & Melancholy.
Take a handfull of Tamarish, one of Agrimony, one of
Wormewood, Century a quarter of a handfull. Boil all theise
in 2 gallons of Wort, & hang them in a bagge wth in ye barrill
wth theise one ounce of Senny, one spoonfull of Anniseeds
Polypode one ounce, Reisons of ye sunne one handfull.
a drame of prepared steel.   mrs Ayres.

67

For a Consumption.

Take 2 spoonefulls of China very thinne sliced
2 spoonefulls of ye White of Hart's-horne very thinne
sliced, 2 spoonefulls of white or redd Saunders thinn
sliced, 4 or 5 spoonefulls of French-Barly well picked
& washed, a Succory root, a Parcely root washed &
ye pith taken out, & sometimes a redd Docke root
picked; putt all theise into 4 pintes of Spring-Water
& into an earthen pott covered & made close to doe.
Let ye pott be sett vpō hotte coales for ye space of
8 or 9 houres: then take more Water & all ye former
ingredients into a bigger pott. Then take a Cocke &
runne him till he be weary, then kill him & dress
him & putt him into ye pott wth 2 spoonefulls of Ca-
pers, some of ye leaues of Borrage, Five-leaud grass,
Rosemary, Violett leaues, Strawberry leaues of theise
every one a little as you can gett them. In
Winter, in stead of herbes, vse Cucumber-seed, Millon
seed, also 2 good spoonefulls of Corrant, 3 of Raisons
of ye Sunne, stoned; when all haue boiled together
for ye space of 7 or 8 houres then take out all ye
stuffe & beat all well in a stone Mortar, then
putt all into the Potte again wth halfe a pinte of White
Wine, & lett it boile awhile, then streim it and
keep it for your vse.

Vse to drinck it thus. Take as much as yu will drinck
& warme it on ye Fire. When it is hotte putt into it a
spoonfull of redd-Rose Water, & a little Sugar,
sometimes a little Conceue of Burrage or Buglosse.

Dr Hunter.

A Jelly

A Jelly for opening y̌ Stomacke & cleansing y̌ Lights.

Take a pottle of running Water, 2 handfulls of Be=
tony of y̌ Wood or Wilde Betony (or for want of it take
garden Betony) one handfull of Unsett Hysop, green
Sage leaues 30, Raisons of y̌ Sunne half a pound, stoned.
Blacke Currants a quartern well washed & bruised in a Mort:
w̌th y̌ Raisons a quartern of fine Sugar, & half an ounce
of White Sugar=Candie to putt into it when it is boyled.
Lett all these be putt into y̌ Water & boile them untill a
pinte of y̌ pottle or somewhat more be consumed. then
putt into y̌ same (whilest it boyleth) a pinte of y̌ best
White Wine, & lett it boyle upp & soe take it off. &
then straine it out & soe Drinck it Euening & Morning
or at any other time finding any stopping.

Pag: 57.9.41

A Caudle to strengthen y̌ Backe.

Take y̌ Pith of an Oxe-back a good quantity, wash
it clean & dry it, take y̌ skinne off & beat it and
straine it w̌th Wine or Ale; take 2 spoonfulls of Oatmeal
searced, y̌ Juice of Comfera, Clary, Knott-grass and
Plantein, take half a pinte of their juice, y̌ Yolkes
of 3 Egges, make it in y̌ forme of a Caudle, season
it w̌th Cinamon & Nuttmeg & Sugar.

For y̌ Jaundize. (M:r Harrison of Yorke's receipt.

Take a quart of old Ale, 2 penniworth of Saffron
one pennyworth of Turnemaricke. Jane's Trracle 2 worth
mingle it togeather till it be well mixed. Make to y̌ quantity
of a Quart & take it at 4 draughts, one at Morne, another
at night, for 2 daies. but when it is to be drunck lett it be
well stirred. / Another for y̌ same. of y̌ La: Cholmely.
Take Rosemary 3 handfulls, a good greene of a handfull of Century.
of Hony half a pinte, put them in 3 quarts of Water, scume it & boyle it
to half, strain it & take 10 or 12 Spoonfulls first in y̌ Morning & last
at night. fast 3 howres after. my La: Rich Cholmeley.

draines.

69

To make Bisskett bread of ye best.

Take ye whites of 10 Egges & ye yolkes of 8; a pound of Sugar, & a pound of flower ye finest ye can gett, being very finely fearced through a Cypress. put ye Egges into a wood Basin & beat them one full houre, & looke there be noe strings in them. & when ye think they be well, putt in ye Sugar by a good spoonefull or 2 at once & soe till ye haue put in all ye Sugar still keeping it continually beating, & when ye haue beaten ye Sugar another houre put in ye flower as ye did ye Sugar by a spoonfull or 2 at once & beat them as before a whole houre. Then put in a little Muske blend wth a little Sugar, & 2 or 3 spoonfulls of Rose water. then putt ye Seedes as many as ye think like. & when ye haue beaten it 3 full hours & ye plates redy rubbd wth a little fresh Butter then you may make them to what fashion ye please & sett them in ye Ouen letting them stand till they be well Baked.

To make Braggot.

Take 6 Gallons of Ale, scarce 3 quarts of Hony being very well claryfied. 2 ounces of Cloues, 2 ounces of Nuttmegs, 2 ounces of Cinamon, 1 ounce of Mace, 1 ounce of Ginger, 1 little spoonfull of Pepper, & half a spoonfull of Grains. Boyle ye Pepper wth ye Hony, & when ye haue boyled it a while putt in all ye Spices saueing ye Cinamon & lett the boyle a little. & when ye Ale hath been twined an houre or 2, & ye Hunny Milke warme, take ye yeast of ye Ale wth ye rind, putt ye Cinamon into ye Hony & blend all together & stirre it in well, Twne it into ye Bundlet & put ye yeast uppe, & let it stand vncouered all ye day then stop it close.

To make Bride

To make Knotts, or Gumballs.

Take 12 yolkes of Egges, & 5 whites. a pound of seareed Sugar, half a pound of Butter washed in Rose water. 3 quarters of an ounce of Mace finely beaten. a little Salt dissolued in rose water. half an ounce of Anice seeds, & half an ounce of Caroway-seed. mingle all these together wth as much flower as will work it up in paste, & soe make it knotts, or rings or what fashion y^u pleafe. Bake them as Bisket bread, but vp^o Pye-plates.

To make Almond-bread, or Fritters.

Take 5 yolkes of Egges & 2 whites, & beat the^m as aforesaid & put in half a pound of seareed Sugar, & soe beat it a q^ter of an howre. then putt in half a pound of flower, & soe beat it half an howre more. then haue ready a pound of Almonds finely beaten wth a little Rosewater, & soe mingle the^m well together, & put them vp^o plates wth a spoon, ye plates being done ouer wth a little Sugar, & soe bake them as ye other Biskett bread, scraping a little fine Sugar vp^o them. Y^u may, yf y^u pleafe, make Fritters in ye same maner, dropping of ye same stuffe with a spoon, vp^o a plate in what forme y^u will. Y^u may, yf you will, put in a quarter of an ounce of Mace finely beaten.

To make Maccarounes, or Fritters.

Take a pound of Almonds, being blanched & beate a pritty while together wth 2 or 3 spoonfulls of Red-rose water. then put in 3 q^ters of a pound of fine Sugar, & beat them together, but not foe fine as for Marchpain stuffe. then take it vp & spread it abroad in a clean Dish & sett it into ye ouen, ontill it be a little hard as y^t top. but y^u must take great heed y^t it browne not. then take it out & stir it very well together, & foe set it in ye ouen again; thus doe 9 or 10 times. then take a grain of Musk, & as much Ambergreece being finely ground, & mingle it well wth ye Almonds & then putt in 4 whites, of new-laid Egges, & soe mingle the^m well together. then when ye ouen is of a good temper, lay them vpon a
plate

71

plate w.th a spoon or cutt them off w.th a slice, Strowing a little
Sugar theron & soe sett them into y.e Ove till they be well hardened
but in any wife they may not browne, but rather lay a sheet of
paper over them, & when they are baked, & well dryed, take them
out. Y.u may make y.f y.u pleafe, Fritters of y.e fame stuffe
dropping it w.th a spoon in what fashion y.u will.

To make fine Cakes.

Take halfe a pound of sheaved Sugar, halfe a pound of sweet Butter
washed in Rofewater, 4 yolkes of Egges & 3 whites. a quarter
of an ounce of Mace, finely beate, a little salt difsolved in
Rofe water, & as much flower as will make it up in pafte,
but it must not be too stuffe. then make y.r Cakes, & prick them,
& soe bake them in an oven upô powder plaits. & yf y.u prick any
y.u must prick the according to y.e worke yf y.u will have them printed
otherwife in what forme y.u will.

To perfume a filver=Bull. or,
to make little Cakes to Perfume.

Take a q.ter of a pound of y.e best couloured Benjamin, pound it fmall
& putt it into y.r bottle to a little Damaske rofe water, mingle it
ontill it be all melted upô y.e fire, & when it is boylô well & com
to a good fmell, y.e Rofe water will part frô it, it must be stird still
in y.e boyling; then when it is boylô enough, put in y.e Mufk halfe an
ounce, & let it boyl a while till all be throughly meltô, be overfure
to have Rofewater in y.e bottle, when y.u fet it on y.e fire to perfume
any place.

For y.e Cakes, y.u must take y.e like quantity of Benjamin, Mufk, &
Civet, but y.u must not fett them on y.e fire, but take Damafk rofe
budds, & cutt off y.e whites & ftamp the very fmall, & then
putt in y.e powder fo providô before, & a little Sugar, foe make
them up in little Cakes, & lay them in a sheet of paper to drye.

An other excellent Perfume to burne.

Take y.e weight of a Groat of Calomes Aromatic, & as much Lignû
Aloes beating it very fine, then put in 2 ounces of Labdanû, halfe
an ounce of Benjamin, halfe an ounce of Storax, 6 graines of Mufk
                                                              6 graines

6 graines of Civitt, & 6 graines of Amber-greece; Beat all theife in a Brass Mortar, & w:th a Brass pestill till they come to a paste. Then wett y:e hand in Rose-water, & worke it up in little round peeces noe bigger then y:u thinke fitting to burne at a time. Y:u may putt into y:e foresaid stuffe a little Damask-rose water in y:e beating & it will worke y:e better.

To dry Apricockes y:e best way.

First gather y:r Apricockes before they be too ripe. then a day after stone them & pare them very thinne, & to a pound of Apricockes take a pound of Sugar. lett y:r Apricockes lye in y:e Sugar covered for 2 howres, untill y:e Sugar be soe moist as it will melt w:thout water. then put y:e Sugar & Apricocks upo a slowe fire, y:t they boyle not in half an hour or more, turning them ofte y:f they breake not. & when y:u thinke they are enough, put y:e Apricocks into some deep glass, & y:e syrope into a silver dish, & let it boyle a little more. poure it on y:e Apricockes, & soe let them stand uncovered untill y:e next day. then cover them & when they have been a weeke in y:e syrope, take them out & lay them on glass plaites, & put them in a stove, or in some cleane place, where they may have y:e aire of y:e fyer, and every day turne them on cleane glasses till they be dry.

How to preserve whole Roses or Gilliflowres or Marrigolds &c. Dippe a Rose in a syrope consisting of Sugar=candy boyled to the full height. then open y:e leaves one by one w:th a smooth bookin of bone, or wood, & as soon as they be dipped lay them in y:e soone when it is in y:e height, or else dry them between 2 dishes upo papers by a very gentle fire & soe keep them all y:e yeare. Y:u must pick y:e seeds out of the:m before y:u doe the:m.

73

To Candy Angelica.

Take yᵉ stalkes in May & boyle them in fair water till yᵉ rinde will pill off. That doe & then make yᵉ Syrop wᵗʰ fair water & Sugar & boyle them in it untill they be tender. Lett them lye in yᵉ same syrope 2 or 3 dayes. Then take them out & pleit them. & Boyling a fresh Syrope to a high Candy-height, putt in yᵉ stalkes & take them p̃sently off yᵉ fyre stirring them too & fro. Then take them forth & lay them on a Pye-plate one by one. & When they are cold Drye them before yᵉ fyre or in a warme Ouen.

An excellent good Perfume.

Take 6 ounces of Benjamin, lay it one night in damask-Rose water. Then beat it & put therto half a pound of damask-Rose leaves beaten also & braid all together. Then mingle it wᵗʰ 10 grains of Muske & 6 of Civett. Then putt in one ounce of hard Suger finely beaten stirre theᵐ together. Then make them into little cakes yᵉ bignes of 2ᵈ Then lay a damask-Rose leaf on either side & sett them in yᵉ Sune to dry.

Mʳˢ Ell: Fairfax.

The Diet drinck

Take Senne   ℥ 4
 Sasaparela   ℥ 3
 Epithmum   ℥ ß
 Hermodactils   ℥ ß
 Sticadose   ℥ j
 Camomell flowers   ℥ ß
 Liquoris ——   ℥ ß

―――――――――――――――

A diet drinke pro morbus

Take lignum Vita   ℥ vm
 Sasaparela   ℥ mj
 Senne   ℥ mj
 amissede   ℥ j
 cologumtida   ℥ ß
 fennell sede & Bentory   ana ℥ j
 Pisule   ℥ ß t
 aqua fontanes   2 4 t
 mallasue   t 1 ß

―――――――――――――――

For the tertian Ague

Auria alexandrina
Oxisaccarum simplex
Sirupus de Acatosa simplex
Sirrop of tart pomgranats
Siropus de Bezantiis.

———————————

For the quarttan Ague

Antidotum asmeritum
Diasene
Mithridatu Andromachi
Oxisaccharum
Unguentu Arogone.

———————————

For the burning Ague

Sirop of Violetts
Diaprunes non laxatiue
Decoction comunis
Electuariu catholicum
Mell Violatum, sirup de lemombz
Trochisio de camphora. Unguentu populion

For the mixt Ague

Diaphenicon
Pilula de agregatiue
Pilula de Rubarbari
Trochisce de diarhodemis ·

––––––––––––––––––––––– ℞

For a longe Ague coming of colde

Diacurcuma
Diacoralium matheſtrale
Pills of Rubarb
Sirupus de Eupatorio
Trochisci de Rubarbario
Trochisci de Absinthio ·

––––––––––––––––––––––– ℞

The 4 greate Whott seedes

Annis seede
Fennell seede
Cummen seede
Caraway seede ·

––––––––––––––––––––––– ℞

The 4 lesser whott seedes

A ny seede
A momiū seede
S malage seede
Y ellow carret sede

———————————————

The 4 greate colde seedes

G ourd seede
C oucomber seede
M illion seede
C ithrone seede

———————————————

The 4 lesser colde seedes .

E ndif seede
S icori seede
L ettue seede
P urflme seede

———————————————

The 4 Whott Vnguents

Vnguentum martiaton Altheam
Vnguentum Aragon
Vnguentum Agrippæ
Vnguentum dialthia

_____

The 4 colde Onpuents

Vnguentum album
Vnguentum Populion
Vnguentum resumtiuum
Vnguentum Citrmum

_____

Fiue Waters to comfort ȳ hart

Endif Water.
Succori Water
Scabius Water
Langdebef Water
Balme Water.

_____

Fiue opening rootes

Smalage rootes
Fennell rootes
Parcely rootes
Sperage rootes
Rue holme rootes

———————————————

Seuen solutiue hearbs

Mallowes,
Mercury
Violatts
Cellworts
Hollihocks
Acanthus
Beetes. //

———————————————

For y bitinge of venomus beast.

Mithridatum
Thriaca galem
Oleum de Scorpione

———————————————

To aſwage paine outwardly

Emplastrum Oxicroceum
Oile of Delle
Oyle of Juniper.

_____

For inwarde diseases

Antidotum Asmeritum
Mithridatum /
Auria Alexandrina.

_____

For burning or skalding

Emplastrum palma
Oile of Mirta /
Unquentu rosatum.
Oyle of egos /
Oyle of Lillies.

_____

for

For appetite

Antidoium asineritum
Aromaticum rosatum
Miua smplex
Conserue of Quinces
Siropp of Wormewood
Eleduarum de comfortiuu stomachum.

For ye colde shaking ague

Muridatum galeni
Sirope of st:cadose
Trochisci de eupatori
Oile of delle
Oile of Sotherne Wood

To comfort a colde brayne

Electuaruu de pemmis
Aromaticuu rosatum
Conserue of gladwen
Thiriaca galeni
Oile of mace.

To purge y^e bladder of grauell

Antidotum Asmeritum
Benedicta Laxatiua
Diacurcuma
Oximel duriticum

_____

To aswage y^e paine in y^e bladder

Emplastrum de oranes Laurelli
Mithridatum galem
Electuarium clusis
Sirup^e de iuiubus
Oleum cheiri
Trochisi de Alchachengi
Oile of sweete almonds.

_____

For the Collick

Antidotum Asmeritum
Aurea Alexandrina
Diaphemcon
Trochisi de Roses
Oyle of camomell

_____

For browses

Emplastrum de Palma
Unguentum aureum
Unguentu Potabile.

———————————————

For pame in spitting

Emplastrum Caromum
Loche de Pino

———————————————

For belching of Winde

Diagalanga
Diatrion peperion.
Diatragacantha calida
Lohoch sanum
Oximele Scilliticum
Sirup de Calaminta.

———————————————

For pame in ỹ back

Pilula fœtida maioris
Oleum de Cheiri
Oleum de Scorpionis
Dia casia .

To drawe forth broken bones

Emplastrum Oxicrocium
Emplistrum contra rupturas

For goute in ỹ feete only

Antidotū asmcritium
Benedicta Laxatiua
Mithridatunι
Pilula de quinῷ oeneribῷ
Mirabolanorum
Pilula fœtida maioris
Oleum Vulpinum
Onguentū marciaton

For ỹ goute .

Rosen or may-buttor make a searcloth ƚæarof æ lay it vpon the
iomment mfit. Brevis e medicina ƥ multū valens æ ƥ omne comptatione.
mr HE Cholmeley.

For to comfort the har:

Diacorallium magistrale
Thiriaca palem
Elect: de gemmis
Sirupl de acetosa
Trochisci de gallium muschata
Aromaticum rosatum
Conserue of roses
Diamber
Dia margaritū calidū:
Diarhodon Abbatis

For ỹ yellow Jaundize

Antidotum asincritum
Diarhodon abatis
Elect: de ribu
Sirop de bizantum
Thiriaca palem
Trochisci de cumphora
Trochisci de rabarbaro
Trochisci eupatorio
Friasandale.

For ye Ellira pashio

Antidotum asmeritum
Theriaca palem
Mithridatum andromachi
Pilula sine quibus
Unguentu martiaton

———————————— ℞ ——

For inflamation

Antidotum asmeritum
Cirotu stomachicum.

———————————— ℞ ——

For whot impostum in the
stomake or liuer ℞

Cirotum stomacho.

———————————— ℞ ——

For inward impossumes

Trochisci de rubarbo
Trochisci de eupatorio
Oleum violarum.

———————————— ℞ ——

For ſ(whot impoſtumes in y throate

Diamoran poti

─────────────────────── ℥─ ──

To ripe Impoſtumes

Emplaſtrũ diachilon magnũ
Empla.ſrũ diachilon parvum
Emplaſtrũ diachilon albũm
Oyle of ʒlewre dilice
Oyle of maſtick

─────────────────────── ℥── ──

For inflomacõn of Choller

Conſerue of Violetts
Unguentũ rosarum

─────────────────────── ℥── ──

For paine of the liuar

Antidotum asincritũ
Diacurcuma
Pilula agregatiui
Pilula eaphorbio
Trochiſci rubarbario
Sirop of Citrac

To make a man Laxatiue

Antidotū esmeritum
Hierapicra galem
Conserue of violetts
Diacasia fistula pro emmatibus

―――――――――――――――

For heate of the Lunges

Diatraganthia frigida
Diardon abbatis
Triasandali
Sirop of violells
Sirop of Endif
Sirop of Endif compounds
Sirop de infusione rosarū devidiarū

―――――――――――――――

For colánes of the Liuar.

Confectio dulcis de muscho
Conserue of mayden-heare
Thiriaca galem
Trochisci absinthio

―――――――――――――――

For y^e hicop

Antidotatum asmeritum
Sirop of mirrh.

_____

For fallinge of y^e heare

Oyle of baye
Oyle of Casse

_____

For ache in the hipps

Auria alexandrina
Pilula fatida maioris
Pilula de gumo generib? mirabon
Oile of baye
Oleum Cuspinum
Unguentu martiaton
Unguentu Arogone

_____

To purge the head

Pilule Aurea.
Pilula cochia rasis

To increase heate in ye inner partes

Antidotum asmeritum
Diacuminu
Diambri
Emplastru stomaticum
Oile of Rew

———————————————

For trembling of ye hart

Confectio de muscho dulcis
Conserue of Borage
Conserue of Longdebeef
Eleosuaru de gemmis

———————————————

For ye heate of the hart

Iulip of Roses
Iulip of violats
Sirop of violats
Sirop of endif compound
Sirop infusione rosaru cindu
Sirope de succo acetosa

———————————————

91

For heate of ỹ liuar

Iulip of Uiolatts
Iulip of roies
Mell Uiolatum
Electuariũ catholicũ
Sirop of Uioletts
Sirop compound of endif
Triasandali
Trochisci de Camphora
Trochisci de spodi
Unguentum rosatum

————————————

To purge ỹ head fuɡ̃. 115.

Pilule Aurea
Pilule cochia rasis

————————————

For the Emrodes

Micleta
Pilula de Bdellio

————————————

For pame of ỹ matrix

Emplastrum de granis lauri
Oyle of sweete almondes.
Trifera
Antidotu asmeritu : good for ỹ mother

_____

For all diseases of ỹ medriff

Mithridatum
Thiriaca galeni
Pelule de cochi rasis
Oile of spike
Oile of euphorbi

_____

For the palsey

Antidotu asmeritum
Canfectio dulcis de muscho.
Mithridatu
Pilule de euphorbio
Sirop of sticados
Vnguentu martiston
Dragorantu frigida

_____

To purge ye Reines of grauell

A ntidotum asmiritum
Benedicte Laxatiue
O ximell duriticum
S irop acctosas compound
S irop of mayden heare
S irop of Citrac

———————————————

For bleeding at ye nose

Trochisci de terra sigilluta
Trochisci de carabo

———————————————

To deliuer a dead childe

Thiriaca galeni
Water of Veruane
Water of sauene

———————————————

To breake the stone

A uria alexandrina
Thiriaca galeni
M ithridatum
O leum de Scorpione

For the faintnes of ý hart

Dia margaritum Calidum
Diasom cum manna
Auria alexandrma
Siren of Sandebese
Conserue of Borage ·//

─────────────────────

To prouoke sweate

Oyle of Delle
Oyle of Cummine ·/

─────────────────────

To stopp sweatt

Rosate nouella
Oyle of Quinces
Oyle of mirts·

─────────────────────

To stae vomiting

Aromaticu gariophilatum
Dia mu simplex
Rosatrta nouellu
Sirop of mints

For $\tilde{y}$ rouphnes of $\tilde{y}$ tongue

Diatraganiha
Diamoron poiio
Sirop of violats.
Oile of sweete almondes
Oile of violatts

━━━━━━━━━━━━

To breake Winde

Antidotum esmeritum.
Aromaticu gariophilatum
Pilule aurea
Diagalanga
Diacurcuma
Electuariu inde maioris
Sirop de eupatorio
Oile of sweete almondes

━━━━━━━━━━━━

For Wormes in $\tilde{y}$ bodye

Pilula contra Lumbricos
Sirop of Lemmons.
Oile of Wormewood
Hira picra galem
Mithredatum
Unguentu contra lumbricos.

unguentū aureum for ulcers or wounds

℞ oyle oliue j lib. ß new waxe j lib. rosme. ℥ iij
therebinthinæ ℥ iij melt all these together then
ade in the collinge franckinsince & masticke
made into very fine poudder anᵃ j. ℥. stiffran
in powder. j. з. mixe them well together & fiat

A strong unguent for an old sore.

℞ hony and whit wyne viniger of the best anᵃ
j pinte verdegrese made in fine powder. j. ℥.
roch allum ℥ ß. boyle all together till it be Reede

A weaker unguent for an old sore.

℞ waxe. oyle. rosin piche. anᵃ j lib. melt them all to
gether & strayne them into a cleane vessell. mixe.
them well till they be colde. and so kepe it to use

An unguent for the Scabb.

℞ enulæ campanæ rotts boyld in stronge viniger
swyns grease & oyle anᵃ ℥ iij wax ℥ ß comon
salt in powder. ℥ ß. terebinthmæ. ℥ iij the Juyce
of fumeterre and lymons of ech half a pinte
boyle all together till the Juyces be consumed
if you will haue it stronger put into it iȷ ℥
of quicke siluer killed in terebinthroz.

A good playstrr for wounds

℞ the Juyce of smallage. planttayn & bettony anᵃ
j pinte wax rosin terebinthine anᵃ lib ß. boyle
all together till the Juyce be consumed & fiat

A playster for old sores

Emplastrū nigrū

℞ read lead made in fine poudder lib j. oyle
lib. ij. viniger. j lib ß boyle all together till
it be black and like a playster & fiat

℞ Dear-sewitt, Red & white-lead of each 3 ounces. sallet oile a pinte.
Bee wax 4 ounces. good white-wine Vineger a pinte Boyle all these
well togeather untill it be blacke &c Dr Butler. Approbat.

116.

To make a clyster.

℞ the rootes of mallowes & lillies. anᵃ ℥ij. iiij figes. the
leaues of mallowes. violets. mercuri. camomyle and dill anᵃ
j ma. aniseed. foenugrece. and lyne seed anᵃ ℥ß. boyle all
these to gether in fresh flesh broth to a pint. when it is
strayned. put ~~benedictum~~ laxatiua & succo rosaru· anᵃ ℥ß. honye &
fresh butter anᵃ ℥j. sweet oyle ℥ij. gene it warme.

A potion purgatiue

Infuse ℥iij of sena. & ℥ij of rubarbe in buglose and
burrage watter anᵃ ℥iiij. a littel stick of cinamon
brused. let them stand all night on whoot embers.
in the morning strame it, and put to it confectionis
hamech. ℥ij. sirup of violets and roses. anᵃ ℥j drinke it
The preparatine to take before is no other thinge
but this. aboue written. but then Leaue out hamech
and take half the sirups. Remember after you
purge you take som comforttabell thinge for
the stomack. as consern of roses. or buglose or quinces

Drunke ye last vp ... wth the roote ... ...
... ... some fowre ... before dynner: and
Keepe ... Birgamer ... ... fowre ... after
... ... or ... ...
... ... at nig ... ...
... ... on ye ... ...
... that some ... of a litle
... ... good bread ... oat some
... ... deram at any ... ...
... sparingly, ... ye Endw/

A clister for ye winde in any part of ye belly or wombe.

In 3 quarters of a pinte of possit-Ale put 2 drames (ye is, ye weight
of 4 groats) of Holland-powder. 3 spoonfulls of sallet oyle, & 3 of
coursa-Sugar. & a little pealt — make it a clister, & take it once,
or twice a weeke.   ye Lа Slingesby.

A glister for ye Iaundize & Ienrvg. &c:

Take a quart of possit-drinke made of small-beare,
putt therin an handfull of Camomill-flowers. Ralfe
a spoonfull of feonell-seeds, or Anice seeds, boyle it fro
a quart to a pinte. putt therto 2 spoonfulls of ye syrop
of Damask-roses. & 2 spoonfulls of powder-Sugar
                                          Dr Bastwick of Yok

for ye same.

Take 6 or 7 Bay berries beat them to powder with 2
pepper cornes & drink it in a cupp of Canary-sacke
an howre or 2 before meat & walk after it./

Or, Take an Orange & eat it skinne & all

Or, Take Broome-ashes & putt them into a potle of
white-wine. keep ye bottle stopped & shake it twice or
thrice a day. then strain it fro ye ashes & drink one
draught in ye morning. & another in ye afternoon, minged
wth a spoonfull of ye Syrop of Succory wherin Rubarb
hath been steeped,

99

18.

A Glister for ye Spleane or mind

Take a pint of Sack and adde unto it one handfull of
Camomile flowers, of lineseeds and Cumiseeds each one ounce
lett them boyle gently till a thirde part be consumed, and then
straine the liquour and put into it the electuarie called diacatho
licon dissolved in the sack and about 2 ounces of the oyle of
dill for a clister to be given warme at anie time of the
day

To make an Earning bage

First let it hang two dayes then wash it very cleane
in faire water and picke the earning that is out of
the Bagg and wash it well in milke and put the
earning into the Bagg againe with two or three
egges new layed being broken shelles and all, and
put to it a little mylke some mace and Cloues and
pepper being beatten and salte to the quantitie of
a nallnott and afterward take a little salt on
the Bagg and hange it to drye then make bryne of
water and salt putting therin a little whole Mace
and Cloues with a leafe or two of ... a little
Clarrie and Sapafridge and then let your bryne
be my could stand and put in your earning bagg to
steep and doe not soe it till two or thre dayes after

To make fine Creame Cheese.

Take fyve quartes of morninges milke and three quartes of euening milke
but put into your Creame poll three or ffower pointes of large
Whaie and put togyur Creame a little earning vnmixled with
two spoune fulls of Rose water and a little of safferon, wospen
it is come take it vp and laye it in the chesfatt without breaking
and presse it downe with your hand then lay it in a fine Cloath
and presse it with a halfe stone weight, and turne it twise or
thrise in six hower then rubb it over with a little salt
and let it drie

To make frefh Cheese

Take a potte of your new milke sodden with ffower egges
continually stirred then put the same into fyve or six pointes
and stirr them well that it breame not then put the same
milke all into one Veffell and put therto some earning as
you doe to an other Cheese, And wospen it is come put among
it Suger Synnomon Rose water And whatt elfe you thinke
good

To make fryed Cruddes and Creame

Take fiue whites of Egges and two yolkes and beate
them together then take a pinte of sweet Creame and
mingle it with them and straine them together and then
put them into a kettle and put to it a braunch of
Rosemary, a nutmedge bruised and a graine of muske
put these in a larone floate and sett it vppon the Ayre
and stirre them well for burning when it beginnes to some
put in the iewse of an Orainge or Lemmon and a little
Rose water and when it is well boyled take it of and let
the vorage runne from it in a faire floate then season
it with suger and boyle the Creame noyse you serueth
vp in with the yolkes of Egges and Rose water

To make Pomanders

Take Ambergreaſe 32 graines muske 11 graines Ciuill
16 graines Beniamin 6 graines Storaches 15
graines Labdanum 6 graines and dragon steept in:
Rose water very thicke and beat them in a stone morter
to strong paste and then mould them

103

To preserue Plombes greene

The best Plombes to preserue greene is the violet date Plombe, the best
time to preserue it in is the latter end of Julie, take a brode skellet
put some fare water in it and sett it on the fier and make it ready to seeth
then put in so many Plombes as will stand one by another and sett
them on the fier, then sett on such another skellett of fare water and make
it boile, and when you see the Plombes a little settled in the first water
take them vp and putt them in the second, then sett on the first water.

and make it boyle againe, and putt them into the water kepping them
close couered all the time of their being in the skellett, but lett them
not boyle till the skim be taken off, then take them vpp and pill of the
thin skim, and sett on the first water againe and make it boyle faster, then
take your Plombes hauing the skim taken of, and putt them into that
water letting them boyle leasurely and being close couered let them boyle
in this liquor till they be as greene as you would haue them, then take
them vp and lay them one by one till the water be cleane runne from th
then weigh your Plombes and to euery pound thereof take a pound and
a quarter of suger finely beaten, putt into the bottom of a brode dis

...ame of your suger and lay in your Plombes one by one, and as you
puft them in rouer or roll them in the Suger, and to a pound puff
halfe a spoonfull of water let them boyle leasurly for 3 quarters
of an houre still turning them in the Sirrupp, then take them from
the fyer and when they be thorough sold puft them vp, and keepe
them neare the heate of the ffier

To make Marmalate of Pippins

Take a pinte of faire water and a pound of Suger boyle and
skim it very cleane, then puft in a pound of Pippins quartered
cored and pared, and let them boyle a prettie while, till they be very
tender, then take them of the fier and breake them in small pieces
with the backe of a Spoone in a Siluer Porindish, then puft them
againe into the Panu and haue reddie two or three oring Pilled,
Being very thinu and finelie cutt, they must first be watered a day or
a night and boyled verie tender, likewise you may puft in the iuce
of 2 or 3 oringes and soe boyle it till it come from the bottom of the
Panu, and then puft it into your Boxes and let them stand souered a
day or two, in some place neare the ayer of the fier, If you haue
not fresh oringes you may take oringe pilles preserued ./.

To make Suger Plate or Losing Comfitts

Take paste a pound of Duble refined Suger finely searsed and putt therto a little gum dragon steeped in Rosewater and a little muske or Ambergreece finely ground, then mingle it woell together in a stone morter till you may worke it like paste then roule it out very thinn and cutt it into little losinges or prinetts, you may make the like with the pouder of Violetts Roses, Marigolds, Elesiorum Cinamon or such like, but in those you shall need neither muske nor Ambergreece, you mayght put into the iuice of Roses a little of the iuice of a lemon to make the colour orient, you may likewise make Sugr Plate with the iuice of clea spik woise or read with the pouder of Brribs

To make Cakes of Apricotts Peare plombes Peares
or Quinces

Take your Apricotts and boyle them but not to murg then scrape the meate from the skin and stone then weigh it with the same waight or more of good Suger, then dry your stuffe in a dish vpon a skin and make your Sirrupp with a little fare onater and Suger and boyle it to the point of manus christi, then boyle all the stuffe togeth and put it vpon plates then sett them in an allmost cold Ouen once or twise and keepe them in a Stour or drying place.

To make A paste of goome

Take rindes of stringo bone pounde, the rindes of Lemoun halfe a pounde water them well, and boyle them till they be tennder then take halfe a pounde of Potatoes or Quinces rosted pounde them together in a Morter putting to them one grane of muske, and a little Rosewater, and when you see them into fine past put to them their weight of fine Sugar finely searced with the weight of an egg, pounde that a new untill you have brought it to fine paste againe, then make it in some Beades to the bignues of a Tennis ball, then put them uppoun oyled tyles into an Ouen and lett them drye but see they catche not to faste, then wash them ouer with the weight of an Egge and Sugar /./

To make quinie Cakes

Boile your Quinces very tender then pare them and take the beste and softest of them, to halfe a pounde of them, take one pounde of sugar beate it finelie and putt unto it as mutch water as will moisten it and lett it boile untill it be reddie to candie, then putt in your quinces and lett them boile together untill it will not stike to your fingers

yninges being well then haue your molde reddie wth a little fine Sugr
sorted vppoun them and see putt on you^r quinces or what thinges
you thinke good and lett them lie vntill they be cold then sett them
before the fier to dry. /./ ./

To make Marlade of Orringes /

Take fare sie rotted Orringes pill them and wringe out the Iuce and
boyle them till they be very tender, shifte you^r wat^r often in the Boyling
till it ceasse to be bitter, when they be boiled tender presse out the
wat^r pard betwene two trenchers, then beat them well in a stone
morter when they be well beaten straine them through a fare searce,
take to every pound of Orringes soe beaten, a pound and a halfe
of Pippins being boiled and strained, then mingle you^r Orringe
stuffe wth you^r pippins and beate them well together wth a spoone.
take the weight of these two togeth^r in Suger being fine lie beatem
and put it into a Pann or Skillett put to it asmuch fare wat^r as will
well moisten it, then set it ouer the fier and let it boile vntill
it come to a manus {christi, then put in you^r Orringe and pippine
stuffe into it and mingle them well together, sett them ouer

PHOTO

108

Ouer the ffier and boile them altogether till it will not stike to your weet
ffinger, then take it vp and make it into Cakes or other deuises as your
selfe shall thinke good :/.·

To make marble Paste :

Take of the aforesaid rolles that you like best and roule it out somewhat
thinn, then take as it were a white and reade flower one vppon another and
putt it out the longer way, and it willbe pillarded like Baroun then sett
one peece by an other and close it the broade way) But you must obserue
to ioyne a white and a read togetther, and your whiten to be somewhat
thicker then your read or other rouled, and when you haue closed it soe sett all
vp, and a peece of the same, then roule it furth both wayes vntill it lake like
iambeste wainscott and soe put it out in peeces or losings: If you will make of
the lesser sorte you must lay your peices one vppon another and roule it vp as
aforesaid and, put it out the longer way) and close one end to another the long
way), then roule it vp againe and putt it sidewayes in little peices
and roule it out, and soe lett it dry :/.·

vide sup
148. 59.

Oyntmente for Aches, Bruses, Cutes, Cuttes, Palsies, Lamenes and Crampes ~ A Green-Oyntment

Take Sage and Rue of each a pound, of wormewood and
Bayes each halfe a pound, Sheeps suett cleane picked three
poundes, Stampe all these together, till none of the suett be
seene, then putt therto one pottle of sweet oyle olive, worke it
very well together then put it into an earthen pott and cover itt
close, And let it stand x dayes, then take it out mouldie as
it is and breake it into a brasse panne and make a softe fi-
vnder it still stirring it, till the herbes waxe sand, then take it
off and lett it coole, and straine it then putt therto two o[z] of
oile of Spike, and stirr it well together and soe putt itt vpp
in Pottes and when you vse it warme it .

To make Sirrupp of Limners

Take Conduit water halfe a pinte, white Suger iiij pounde
Boile them together till halfe the water be consumed, then put o

PHOTO

them a q^{te} of a pinte of white wine vinnyer, and lett them all
boile againe togetter contill they)come vnto the consistance
of a Sirrupp still takinge awaie the Skime verie cleane

To make Almond Ginger-bread

Take foure score Almondes blanch them in faire wat^s warme
but put them p^rsentlie into fare colde wat^s as you blanch
them tie the Almonde in a fare linnyng cloth and beate them in a
stone Morter a verie little wosite, then put two or three spoonefull
of bread Rosewat^s to keepe them from oilewing this done you must
beate them very)neare an houre, and put in that quantitie of
Sugar finelie searced that you thinke will make it sweet enoug
it must be beet exceedeing finelie, and euer as you beate it put all
in Cinamon and Ginger finelie searced, when it is sufficientlie
beaten mould it and printe it in Cinamonde and Ginger but
noe Suger, when it is made it must be keept vpon paper in
a Box)neare the fier. /././

To make ~ Pippins ~ Puddinge ~

Take a halfe crindle, a quart of Creame, halfe a
dozen Egges, a Manchett, a pound of Currans, w[i]th Cina
mon, Ginger, Nuttmegge, mace and Cloues, and Suger,
and a little rose woat[er], a quantity of sope meriorum,
penny riall, winter Sauory, and Camomill shred all these
small w[i]th some mutton suett enough, putt them into
the Bagg and soe boile itt.

To make ~ Sauedges ~

Take the fillett of ~ Porke w[i]th some other parte thereof
that is fatt and leane well mixt and not Sinowey, mince
then put it into a morter, w[i]th a little small bett Cloues a
mace, a little quantitie of grosse pepper, and nuttmeg
beaten, Sage winter Sauory, and time mince them
smale, then put them togethere w[i]th soe much salte as it
fitt for the seasoning, then lett them be well beaten p[ut]

Putting hereto the yolkes of three egges or more according
to the quantitie of your stuffe, after ( ) beating, if
it doe not appeare fatt enough, mince some beefe suett
and putto it yp ropes being steept a day) or a night in
rosite roine, then make them vpp ././

To make ffine Suett ././

Take the kydney of fine mutton Suett or lambe, and
pitt it cleane and beate it wth a woodden Pestell in a
Marble morter, then put it into a fine earthen Pipkin
and two marij mallow rootes cleane pitked wth the
pith taken out and brused and stopp vp the Pipkin
and let it boile vpon embere, then straine it and beat
it wth may due of a yeare olde into a purslland dishe

To make a Skirrett Pie ././

Boile and pill yp Skirrets and put them into yp
paste, and season them wth Nutmegge a litle pepper
and rosole Mace, and a quarter of a pounde of

of Suger and a few berberies, then take the marrow
of the bones beng broken, and put them in colde water
then take the yolkes of three egges beaten and put the
marrow into it, and rowle it up in the egges till it
haue taken all up and soe lie it into yor paste, then take
a quarter of a pound of dates and cutt them take out
the stones and the white, and put them in, then take sweet
butter brake it ouer all your dates with it, and soe close
it up and after it is baked take a penny poll of white wine
a muge of white wine viniger, a quarter of a pound of
melted butter and a quarter of a pound of Suger mix
all these well together and poure into yor Pie and soe
serue itt

To rost a Shoulder of Mutton. /

Take a shoulder of good mutton, and take halfe a pecke of good Oysters
wash them well and draine the water cleane from them, take the
toppes of Rosemary, time, and Persley chopp them small, also the

the yolkes of three hard egges wth a Lemonn and an Onion minced
altogether, putto a quantity of grosse pepper, and fower spoonefull's of
wine viniger mingle all these together wth your Oisters, then stuffe the
shoulder of mutton being fare washed therwth, and baste it wth sweet
butter, when it is rosted take 4 spoonefull's of white wine viniger
and put it to some of the gravie and soe serue it. /./.

To boile a Carpe

Take a good Carpe and rub his sticke, take out the gall from the
liuer, then put the scroticye in his barke, take salte and scoure him
very well, and wash him in fare water, take then halfe a pinte
of wine viniger halfe a pinte of white wine halfe the skyn of
a Lemon, two fare races of Ginger slicet halfe a quarter
of an ounce of Large mace, a fewe toppes of time, and
rosemarie, wth halfe a pound of sweete Butter, put all these
into a deepe dish that will containe your Carpe, put in three
spoonefull's of salte, set it on a Chafindish of Coleb till
it boile, and then drie your Carpe very fare, and put into
the

the dish, and power him; and lett him boile a quarter of
an houre, then turne him, and put in a quantity of more
salt, let him boile another quarter of an houre, then take
a manchette and put in, toasted, and either toast them or fry
them, and lye them in a faire dish, take alsoe a quarter
of a pound of sweete butter, fower spoonefulls of wine
vineger stirre them together till the butter be melted, then
take the Carpe out of the broth, and lie him vpon yor
Sippetts, and poure yor sauce theron, with a good quantity of beaten ginger strowed vpon it, and soe serue it.//

To make Puffes.

Take a Porrenger full of Egs curde and brake into them
Fower Egges, then putto them a handfull of muscate flower
and Nutmegge, and make them vp into little Loues
and set into the Ouen vpon a paper being well rubbed

rubbed with Butter, and serue them vp with butter

and suger ./././

To make Pantables ./.

Take six Egge yolkes and a pinte of Creame and

halfe a pinte of wate, Nuttmegges and suger as

much as will season itt make your Batter of a reasonable

thicknes with fflower and soe frye them

To Cramm Capons ./.

Take ffine wheate meale and mingle it with suger

or hony) and soe make itt into Rowles, and soe you

may) make a Capon fatt in six dayes. But the

wheate meale must be moulded with Butter or

Sewett ./././

To make Manus Christi.

Take half a pound of refined Sugar, & some Rose-water, & boyl it till it come to Sugar againe. Then stirre it a little about & putt in y̆ Leaf-gold: then cast it according to Art into little round gobletts, & soe keep them.

To make paste of Quinces, Plumbes or Barberies.

Straim y̆ pulp & take y̆ weight in Suger, & boyl it till it be as thick as it may stand on a Pye-plate, & fashion it some like Leaves & some like Plumes w̆ their stones & stalkes in them. Then put thē in a warme Ouen, when it is hard & drye. then turne them & dry y̆ other side in an ouen after y̆ bread is drawn. then being kept dry y̆ may keep thē all y̆ yeare.

To make Paste-royall of Marmelade.

Take of this paste & molde it vp in searced Suger till it come to perfect paste. then print it w̆th y̆ Mouldes & drye it in an Oue after y̆ bread is drawne. then box it vp being drye. If they chance to be moysd dry them in an Ouen again as before.

To make Paste of Genua.

Take of y̆ pulp of Quinces or as much of Peaches & straim it & dry it in a Platter vpō a chafing dish of coales. then take y̆ same quantity of Sugar & boyl it to y̆ Right of Manus Christi. then lay it vpō a Pye-plate and fashiō it as y̆ please. & soe dry thē in an Oue as y̆ other before.

To make paste of Pippins.

Take y̆ Pippins pare them & quarter thē, then boyl them in faire water till they be tender then strain them & dry y̆ pulp vpō a chafing dish of coles. then weigh it & take as much Suger as it weigheth & boyl it to Manus Christi & putt thē together. then fashion them vpō a Pye-plate & putt them in an Oue being very slenderly heat. y̆ next morning y̆ may turne thē vpō y̆ bottom of a siue w̆th paper vnder them, & soe putt them in an Ouen of y̆ same heat again. & there lett them remain 4 or 5 dayes putting every day a chafing-dish of coles into y̆ Oue till they be dry.

to bake venison in a
good crust

Take yo side, or fouchef venison &
wipe it w a cloth, ye bones being out,
say it fitt for yo pasty, sasson it with
peper & salt. lay it in prefse, if yo please
2 or 3 days; then take to a peck of fine
wheat flour. 4 pound of butter, broken
into litle bits & soe wrought to ye very
w ye flour, lay it a-brode of ye table &
take 18 eggs butt 9 of ye whits, & soe
worke them in very well, then sprinkle
cold watter & still work it till it be well
in stifnefs, pluke it in litle peeces 3 or 4 Tims over
& then mould it & roll it fitt for your
pasty, laying minched suitt under ye
meat, & a narrow peece of past a-bout it

a roste a
gge of
veal.

Take ye fatt of ye kidnee of a loin of veil & cutt it in
litle long peeces, role it in Nottmoge & salt mingled
together, stof yo lege of veil w it & w earbes, but
make ye holes deeper. prick a peef of kell over it.
ye saffs is butter & viziket Nugmoge salt
& a little suger. cutt offe ye bone end & sene
it up-right.

to make puffe past

Take a quantety of fine flower -
4 whits of eggs, a little rose water
or other cold watter, mold ye past
together & beat it wth ye rolinpin, for
ye stiffer yo make it, ye better, then rol
rolle ye past forth & lay ye butter on
in bitts, turne it up of both sids & so
do it 4 or 5 times & then make it up.
ye may lay a bitt of a little paper & so
sett it in ye oven to se if it rise,

ye must be sure to beat yo
butter, wth a rolinpin, till ye watter
be very clean forth of itt,

a nother way
Take a pound butter & a pound of fine flowr
2 whits eges, as much watter as will make yo
past very stiff, then rol it oot, & spread yo
butter on it all one way & strow a little floor
over it & rol it up and close the butter in &
so do yo butter 4 or 5 times as yoo did before,
work yo butter & lay it in.
watter o ovr night to
make it stiff

to set on a floor in time with the
kidney of veal

Take yo kidney shred it smal; 2 Aples shred —
them smal; 2 eges; little softwater; sinamon
nott mouch some suger; a little cream, & son
candid oringpils cutt smal, corrans & rijons,
a date or tow; if yo pleseth;

To make Gingerbread by Josh Ropers Rect
Take 4 pound of Treacle, 1 oz of Carraway
seeds, 1 oz of powdered ginger a slice
of butter, mix these severally into
3d 4d of flower, adding ½ pd of Orange
& Citron sliced — mix with ye Treackle
2 spoonfuls of good yest & 3 spoonfulls
of brandy. and work these altogether
Just before you set it into ye Oven
butter & flodrr ye Tin pan ———
It will take an hour & half. or two hours.
Baking ————

140.

Another Ginger bread Cake ——

To three pound & an half of flower
put 3 pounds & an half of Treacle,
Two ounces of Ginger finely beaten
and sifted one Ounce of sweet Fennel
seeds Do Carraway seed bruised four
spoonfulls of Sack Do brandy. add a little
zest The Oven must not be too hot
It will take an hour & an half baking   *or two hours*

Another Which my master Davison liked best
for his pocket when an hunting ——

To 3 pounds of Flower mix one ounce of ging.r
1oz of Carraweyseeds. 1oz of Corriander Seeds beat fine
then these severally with the flower, and add a good
slice of Butter. Then take Two pounds & three pts.
of Treacle mix into it Two or three spoonfulls
of yest & 3 Spoonfulls of Brandy & ½ pound
of Orange peal ——   Bake it
Two hours at least ——

A note howe to dis blewe
· out off whithe ·/

Inp: thike: 12: gallans off thambur̄be
be left it on the fire; then when it
is almost at boylinge, thike then
skumbe cleane off it, and then
thike it off the fire, and lett it sattle
then cleare it, and thike a q3th off
a pound off indico, mingle them to
gether, then thike no cloth or woole
or any other thinge dieable, and stirr
them verie well about for feare off
spottinge./

Howe to dis poreiniaye
grene, out off whithe,

Inp: To vij off woole; thike one
pounde off allome; Boyle fayre
water, and when it is at boylinge
put no allome unto it, which beinge
melted, put the woole into it, and so
boyle them together, for the space off
three houres, then thike it off the fire
and coole it, and put out all that
water; then thike more faire water
and grene grasse; and boyle them
togither one houre, and then thike
out the grene grasse and put no

PHOTO

123

wooll into that watter, let them boyle for
out qȝter off an houre, and then taike it
vp, And wringe it verie harde, and put
it into ye blewe fatt. /

How to dy a feuerȝ grene /

firſt maike it a good blewe, then waſſe
it vp in faire watter, then taike al Rome
ſtronninge to the firſt proportion. And boyle
it thre houres, allwaies when yo vſe any
allome, then taike it vp. then taike faire
watter, and grene graſſe, and boyle them
an houre togiders then taike out ye grene
graſſe, and put halfe a gallan off chamberls
into ye grene graſſe watter, and then
put the wooll into it, and ſtirre it about
for feare off ſpottinge, iſ it be wooll
wringe it and waſſe it, iſ it be cloſſe
hange it vp, vntill it be wele don then
ou aſſe it. /

How to dy a watered
~~chollons~~/
Fyr: put yo[u] ~~chollons~~ woole into the
blow fatt; and make it a reasnable
blewe; then wringe it vp and washe
it; then taike faire watter, and a litle
allome, (w[i]t[h] melter) put them toge[ther]
boyle them one houre; and so taike it
vp and washe it; /

How to dy a seawater grene
first yo[u] must blewe it; and wringe it vp
then taike a poun[d] of Logwood; and eight
yardes of clothe; and boyle it with
grene grasse; and allome; thre houres
then roole it; and then it wille a sea
grene!! / So far blew will make a far
greene /

How to dy a maiden haire
colour out of white;

Taike one pound of allome; and wisp
of woole; boyle them in faire watter
thre houres; then taike forte th[a]t
water; and put in faire watter and
grene grasse; and boyle them an houre
then taike out all the grene grasse and
put in rotten tree; and halfe a gallan
of chamberlea; and boyle them toget[her]
v[n]till yo[u] thinke it be a faire colour;

How to dye a bright stamell ingrane
out of white

Taike 4 pound ash. Allome to y⁰ send
proportione off wooll, and boyle it in faire
water three houers, then taike it fourth
and wasse it veris faire, then tuike faire
water, and then taike thre ounres off
ffuttrgoneals, well beaten to smale powder
and one pennyworth off arssnicke, and two
pennyworth off mirtuvas, beat them all
stmall, and put them all togeth⁰ off a
powder diffe irie, and mingle them
with one spoonfull off wheat floure, and
then divid them into two yole, then
taike one off the yole, and put them
into y⁰ faire water, when it is almost
hate, and then stirre it well, and then
put in y⁰ woolle, and let them boyle
halfe an houre, then taike yt fourth
and roole it, and when y⁰ woole or
clote is roole put in thofe yole, off y⁰
ffuffe into that water, and stirre it
well, then put y⁰ woole or cloth into
that water ygaine, & let it boyle hulfe
an houre, then yⁱ may se when the
colle is faire, and so taike it up
wasshng it very well ./
5

To make a faire skarlitt out
off whit for sower yeards

Take faire water, and when it is at boylinge, put halfe a peck off wheat brane
to it, let it boyle halfe a q3tr off an houre
then put it into some tubbe for a fortnight
to make sower, and every day stirre it
about, then take faire water and set
it on the fire, and put some off ye sower
brane water unto it, then when it
boyleth, put 1lb off allome unto itr
then put in 1lb clofse az woole and
let them boyle togither thre houres, then
take it upp and coole it, then put out
that water, and take the rest off ye
brane water, and ^one gallon or two off
smale drinke or dropinge, then put
in ye cloth or woole into that, and let
it boyle togither one q3tr off an houre,
then take it up and coole it, then
take thre ounces off suttergencale
one pennyworth off mrurras, one
pennyworth off arsnicke, one penny
worth off orpinll, beate them sevrallie

verie smale then mixte them togither
then take one q{rt} off a pownd off farra-
nand: purke, and put them all togither
into the said mixter, and then put in yo
cloth or wooll, stirringe them verie
well, and soe let them boyle for halfe
an houre, for feare off spottinge, and
then take it up and roole it, then
put into that likquor, aqts off a
gallan off chamberlea, stirr it well,
and put yo cloth or wooll in againe halfe
an houre, but in any case stirr it well
well, and then take it up and roole it
and beinge colde washe it verie faire/

How to dye a purple ingraine

first make it a good blew, then allome
it for 3 houres, then washe it up, and
put it into the skamell likquor aboue
said, and when yo thinke it faire take
it up./

for a watchet draw it through
yo skamell fatt then blew it then
boyle it in allome,/

PHOTO

To dye yallow: take crabtre barke
and boyle it an houre in faire water
and then take vp ye barke, yf yt be for
a dosen off clote, a pownd & a halfe off
allume, boyle it & ye clote in that
lickquor, bothe togethr, one houre./
yf ye will have a stravt collor put
in maystrenge to it /
yf a goli my yallowe take it furst
and put in a skoole full off chamber
loa, and stirre but about and then
take it forth, & put it into ye
hoote lickquor againe, and stirre
it but about and take it forth
againe then drie it & wasse it
after it be drie at yo laysure /
                    vyolet
for purpole ~~velvet~~, take a pownd off
Alkonie for vij yourds off clote
and boyle it, in it, for her & houris
[?] forth ye allome water, and
wasse ye vessell clene, and then-
fill it full off faire water, then
take a pownd off logwood, in skitt-
thencalo, & and when it is
very warme then put it in, then
let ye logwood boyle a gst ?off an

houre then take yᵉ cloth and put
it in, and let it be in till it be very
[...], and stirie it well for feare
of spotinge)

To whiten fine yarn, or cloth;

Take a quantity of chamberlye according to yᵉ larg-
ness of yᵉ web, & put in as much new cowe dounge, as in
yᵉ descreation yᵉ thinke will suaue, then mingle well
wᵗ yᵉ chamberlye, & rob it well wᵗ yᵒ hands, till all the
lomps be broken, then lay in yᵒ web when yᵒ have
washt it out of yᵉ souling & dryed it, & soe lett it lye
yᵉ space of 2 dayes, & 2 nights, then take it out & wash
yᵉ cowe-douge cline frō it in fair watter., then lay it
forth a day, & a night, & turn it & soe lett it lye again
a day & a night, alwayes watering it, soe that it
never dry, then wash it cline in fair watter, & hat
it & lay it in a boking tubb, then lay on yᵒ Ashcloth
& take yᵒ Ashjis & boyl them in fair watter, & soe pour
them on & soe lett it stand all night, in yᵉ morning drive
it & bat it out, & soe lay it out as before, yᵒ mᵘ remember that every day yᵒ bat it but in fair watter
& Sow a little pece of cloth on yᵒ ons side of it, wherby yᵉ
may know to turn it right, this yᵒ may doe twise or
thrise, both for laying of it in yᵉ cowe-douge & for
boking of it; yᵒ Ashjis must be ether of thistles,
brukens, whinss, or Ashe; all must be burnt before they be
[...] though dry

154

likewife your yarn most first be washed out of the
Sowling, ther take a good quantity of Ashes in boyle
them well in a kettle till the strength of ye Ashes be in
the watter, then take it of & lett it stand till ye
Ashes be all settled to ye bottom, then take clear
therof & boyle your yarn therin, the space of a-
houre, & lay it out in ye Lay 2 days & 2 nights, watering it very well, soe that it never be thorow
dry, then batt it up in fair water, & soe dry it;

a nother way to whiten
cloth, or yarn.

Take a pound of burnt Allohlaster, finely beaten
& put it into warm watter, & steer it well together
then take 20 yeards of cloth, weight out of ye sowling
then lay in yo limme with as much watter as will
cover it & lett yo limme lye in this watter, 24 howers
stirring it 3 or 4 times, during the time it lyeth in
this liquor, then lay it forth in fair wether & watter
it 2 or 3 days, then bucke it, that done lay it forth,
& watter it 2 or 3 days againe, then lay it in your
whiting 24 howers more as aforesade stirring
it 2 or 3 times, and at your discretion dry it up, &
shall it need small batting;

for yo yarn take ye same liquor as aforesade so
shall you nott need to seeth yo yarn.)

lay in yo yarn the space of 2 days & 2 nights, then
lay it out, wash it forth & dry it without anie
beating & after it is whited 2 or 3 days, lay it in
the like liquor 24 howers more, & take it and
make it fitt;

Doctor Stephens water *as I heard of Archbishop of Canterbury*

given it of him a little before his death. *he my brother his Chaplaine? could certifie*

Take a gallon of Gasscoigne wine, ginger, gallingall,
Cinnamon, nutmegs, Cardamon, graines, Cloves, Annisseeds,
fennell seede, carraway seede, of every of them a dramme,
then take sage, mintes, redrose, time, pollitorie, rossmarie,
wilde time, Cammomile, and lavander, of everie one of
them a handfull, then bray the spices and hearbes, and
put all into the wine and let it stand for twelve howers
stirre it divers times then distill it in a Lim beck
and keepe the first water by it selfe for it is the best
And keepe alsoe the second water which is good, but not
like the first./

To make vsquabaughe

Take a quarter of a pound of Liquorice, scrape it cleane
and bruise it, and cutt it into small peeces, then take a
quarter of a pound of rasins of the sunne, and stone them
a quarter of a pound of dates, cutt and washt verie cleane
then take a good spoonfull of Annisseeds bruised, then put
all these in 3 quartes of Aqua vitæ, and soe lett it steepe
24 howers, shaking it 3 or 4 times, then put it from the
ingredients into a bason, put as much Suger to it as will
give it a pleasante taste, then let it raine through a
Jelly bagge once or twice, and soe keepe it

Another way to make vskabaughe

Vskabaugh.

Take a pottle of Aqua vitæ, and therein steepe, of Sinamon mace, and cloues, a quarter of an ounce, and of nutmegs and ginger of each halfe an ounce, of Carraway and Colleander seeds halfe an ounce of each, of liquorice sliced two ounces of raisins of the sonne a quarter of a pound, put into it two rootes of Elacompana, Succorie, Cumfrey and fenill a little muske, and two ounces of suger candie, lett all these lie in steepe fower or fiue daies, and lett it runne through a cotten strainer. /

To make rosa solis
see pag 160.

Take a pottle of the best aqua composita, put it into a gallon glasse, and put therto a pottle of the hearbe called rosa solis cleane picked, and lett it stand three or fower dayes close stopped then take one ounce of ginger bruisd, one ounce of Cinemon bruisd a quarter of an ounce of whole mace, two spoonfulls of Aniseeds bruised, a round of white suger Candie, and 20 dates cutt in small peeces, and put them into another gallon glasse, and put therto your aquacomposita, strained from your rosa solis, and soe lett it stand vntill you haue occasion to vse the same. /

To make aqua mirabilis

Take Gallingall, Cloues, qui bibis, ginger, melito cardimomia mace, nutmegs, saffron, agremonie, of each of these one drame and of the Iuce of sallindine.

To make Vshabaughe.

Take a Gallon of White Aqua-composita & putt it in a Vessell.
then take a pound of Musk-comfetts; an Ounce of Cynamon, 3
stickes of Lycoris, & an Ounce of fine Sugar. Bruise all these
& putt the to y͠e Aquavite & let them remain there 12 daies. and
stirre the well every day, & then powre forth y͠e Syrop fr͠o the rest
as clean as you may.   & this is y͠e perfect Vshabaugh.

An excellent drinck agt y͠e Plague

For. Mashedine.

Take 3 pintes of Malmesy, an handfull of red Sage, as much of Rue,
boyle these to a quart then straine out y͠e hearbes, then take an ounce of long-
Pepper ginger & Nutmegs all beaten small in a Morter & put into y͠e Wine
& boyle it a little, then take it off & putt into it an ounce of Methridat

For. Rott Angelica Root.

2 ounces of y͠e best Treacle, & a quarter of a pinte of Aquavite, & putt
all into y͠e Wine & soe keep it. | How this is to be Vsed
Any y͠t feare y͠e Plague & are not Infected, may take 2 a much halfe a
spoonefull of this drinck at a time. & If any be Infected take a spoonfull
of it (as soon as y͠e party thinketh himself infected) luke warm & soe goe
to bed & sweat 2 or 3 howres, & then dry y͠e body well & keep warme
& drinck noe cold drinck but warme drinck & caudles, & posset drinck
w͠th Marigold leaues & flowres, when y͠e party hath sweat, & is well dryed
w͠th warme clothes, & soe long as y͠e party is ill take a spoonfull Morning
& euening.
                                     M͠r Ruskin his Receipe.   or D͠r Burges.

Another for y͠e same.

Take red Bramble leaues, Sage, Rue, Elder leaues of each
one handfull. straine y͠e iuice into a quart of White Wine. take
2 spoonfulls once in a weeke.
                            m͠r Gu.

To cleanse an infected Howse.

Stoppe vp y͠e chimneys & windowes. then take tallowe, tarre, pitch
soot & vineger boyl these in an earthen-pott vpon a chafing dish
of coales & make a perfume.
                            y͠e La: Selby

for y Ricketts, (in children.)

Take Succory, Colts-foot, Scurvigrass, Liang-worte, Fumiterorge,
Sanicle, Hey Ryse stamp them set y juices over y fyer, clarify it wth
whites of Egges, then strain it againe, put to every pinte of juice
a pound or a halfe of fine Sugar, boyle it according as y doe boile
other Syropps, giue y childe a spoonefull morning first or during last

y Ointment, / Take Camomill, Sage, Lavender, Hissope,
Mavish, fetherfew, Heyhise, Organum, Sanicle, redd fennill, wormewood, Spere-mynt, Saint Agofers herbs choppe them all small: boile
them in fresh butter, put in a large-Mace or halfe a pinte of
Muskedime, when it is boyled strain it or keep it for y vse.
y childe must be anointed morning or euening; back, sides or Reines
or after rouble or tumble it.

If y child canot contein what it taketh: Take Spere-mynte
small chopt, or Cloues beaten, boyle theise in Muskedime or vineger
or applye it to y stomack or vpper part of y belly.

A water vsed to mixe wth y Syrope. for rich folkes.
Take a fatt sucking Pigge, dress him or spitt him, or when it is halfe roasted
cutt him in pieces, putt it into a gallon of new Milke, putt thereto the
crombs of a penny-white-Loafe, a pound of dates stoned, an ounce of
Rine-apple Kirnells bruised, a quarter of a pound of Almonds Blanched
or beaten, a pound of Lent-figges cutt in pieces, halfe a pounde of
Raisons of y sunne stoned, a pound of Coranee washed, a Handfull
of Spicedwell, y like of Burnett, Betony, Scurvygrass, 30 or 40 garden
Snailes well cleansed, put all theise in steep 4 howres or then still it
in a comon still, take this water in a quart glass into which y
must putt 6 leaves of golde, putt white-Amber powdered 2 dragms
prepared Pearle 3 dragmes, stirre theise well together or mixe it
wth the Syrope, If the childe be farre spent for y poorest sort
(3 lb to) take garden Snailes or putt in a little redd Rose water
or Sugar, or giue y childe to drinck 3 times a weeke. feb. 25. 1632.

my La: Fairfax of Street

For a Consumption.

Take a peck of Turneps clean washed & dryed again either by ye sun
or fire, slice them & putt them in a new earthen pott close stopped.
lett it in ye Ouen about one hower & a halfe. then straine out ye juice,
& to every pinte of syrope putt a pound of Sugar. Boyle it to a Syrop
height. take 4 spoonefulls in ye morneing first & as much at night last.

my La: Exiter.

For ye Fame.

Take 3 quarts of spring water & put a calfes foot in it. 3 ounces
of Harts-horn, one ounce of Cinamo broken. Boyle all theise together
unto 3 pintes. then take out ye Calues-foot & put in half a pinte of
red Rose water & a pinte of Muskedine, & 2 ounces of Sugar, & lett
them boyle a little all together. & then put it into a pott. & take of it
3 or 4 spoonfulls every morneing, & in ye day time now & then a spoonefl
& at night.—

To Mrs M. Asheto.

For ye Palsey

Take a pottle of old Ale without Hopps, half an ounce of Nuttmegs, a qter
of an ounce of ginger, half a quarter of an ounce of Cinamo, & half
a qter of a pound of Sugar. beat ye spices together in a mortar. putt
them in ye ale: & take a quarter of a pound of Tionge-root & bruise
it in ye mortar, & putt into ye ale & spices, & lett it stand 3 nights
& then drinck it ye morneings. Stirr it well together & ye drinck it.

mary watson.

To bring away an After-Birth.

Take yellow Amber as much as a bean & knock it small, and as
much Hartes-horn as will lye on 2^d. & a little Beavor-stone on ye point
of ye knife. yf ye haue it not, then make it strong of Amber. & ye must
take 4 or 5 spoonfulls of womans-Milk & mingle all together wth as
much speed as ye can to ye party. & let ye party first clean off in
her bed, & ye midwife to be wth her, & hold fast ye string, & wash
ye party in warme water ye first thing shee dosh when is kneeled
vp in her bed. & then lett ye party lett down her breath in y^e
midwifes hand &c:

To Mrs M. Asheton.

For yͤ Backe. &c:

Take yͤ pith of an Oac & take yͤ shrane or filth away. yͤ wͨ is good of it when it is beaten shinne putt it into 2 quarts of Ale. boyle yͤ ⅓ part away. then take liue-stony finely clarifyed & putt 2 good spoonfulls in it at yͤ first, & frason it more as yͤ will haue it of Sugar, & white-bread Coumbs finely grated alsbury like. 8 or 9 Dates stoned & sliced & putt in at yͤ first. a few whole Cloues & a pretty deal of white Mace, & boyl them all together. take 12 spoonfulls in yͤ morning, & 5 or 6 at night. but be sure to eate yͤ pith. Eate noe Veal, nor Pigge, nor any slimy meat.

Mͬˢ Askew.

Ros-solis. (see sup. 15b.

This herbe groweth in medotwes or in lowe moorish-grounds, & in noe other place. it is of hoare colour & groweth very lowe & flatt to yͤ ground. It hath a meane long stalk growing in yͤ midst of it. & 6 brunches springing out of yͤ root round about yͤ stalk & leaues of mean length & breadth. In noe wise when it is gathered let it be touched wͭh yͤ hands, for then yͤ virtue therof is gonne. yͤ must pluck it vp by yͤ stalke, & lay it in a clean baskett, for yͤ leaues therof are of very much nature.

Take as much of this herbe as will fill a pottle-pott or glass, wash it not in any wise. then take a pottle of Aqua-composita & putt them both in a large pott or vessell, & lett it stand hard stopped 3 dayes & 3 nights, & yͤ 4 day open it & strain it through a fair linnen cloath into a clean glass or pewter pott, & putt thereto a pound of Sugar-beaten small. halfe a pound of Licorise beaten in fine powder. halfe a pound of Dates cutt in small pieces, and mixe them all together. & stopp yͤ pott or glass for yͤ noe aire come in. then drinck to bed-ward halfe a spoonfull mixed wͭh a quantity of good stale Ale, & as much in yͤ morning fasting. And there is not the weakest body in yͤ world yͭ is wasted in Consumption or otherwise but it will restore them again. & cause them to be strong & lusty, & to haue a maruelous stomach. And yͤ shortly they yͭ vse this receit 3 times together, shall finde great remedy & comfort therby. And for as yͤ patient findeth himselfe, for hee may vse it. Note also yͭ this herbe Ros-solis can not nor may not be gathered but onely in June or July.

Hͬ Cholmeley.

For ye Head-acke.

Rx Herbe-grace & Fennell & boile them together, & lay it to ye stomack. and
use it till then be whole. / for ye same. Rx Rosmary, Camomill,
Violetts ana M i. boyle them tenderly in white-wine & binde ye Robes plaisters-
wise about ye patients head. / A purge for ye same. Rx Pelitory of
Spain & strue ye root thereof into Ale & drink it. It shall purge ye heade
& take away ye acke, & fasten ye teeth well. Probatum est. H.C.

To make a Worme come out of ye Head.

Take ye marrow of a Bull or Cowe & putt it warme into ye eare, & ye worm
will come forth for sweetness of ye marrowe.

For giddyness in ye head of long continuance.

Rx ye gall of an Hare & as much of Hony & mingle them together a good space
untill it fall to a curde, & therewith anoynt ye forehead & temples.

For Deafness.

Rx Oile of Anyse-seede & bitter-Almonds mixed together, & putt 3 dropps
into ye eares warme, & stopp it wth black woll.
Or take Oile of Comyn. it hath been proved good.
Or ye juice of Colewoort mingled wth Wine & drop it into ye eares.
Or Rx ye gall of a Hare, Aqua-vitæ & Womans-milk ana pt after. & drop it in.
Or ye Urine of a young man-childe new made. Or Rx ye juyce of Rue wth ye s'd Urine

To help any man being simple of hearing, yt hath been so of long time

Take young Ash-wood make a fagget thereof & lay it on ye fyre then take ye water
yt droppeth out of ye ends thereof & putt thereto ye greaseof a silver-coloured Eell. then
bruise a little Comyn & steep it in ye grease & Ashwater & putt thereto a little
vineger & let it stand for one night. then put to it Castori a penny. weight,
& being well steeped let ye liquor runne through a linen cloath. then putt a
drop or more into ye eare it being clear & warme. then dipp black woll in it
& stop ye eare therewth. & let ye patient lye on ye contrary side & it will restore
ye hearing again by God's help.

To make a man Hear yt ever he shall heare.

Take a great Onyon & cutt off ye upper-part & then take away ye coar. then
fill ye Onyon wth Oyle-olife & cover it again wth ye part cutt off, & sett ye Onyon
in ye hotte imbers. & lett it boyle well. then when thou goest to bed, lett ye Oyle
be dropt into thine eare. (yt wch is upmost) as hott as thou maist suffer it. & lye still
& sleep. & use it for 3 or 4 times when ye awake glow.

Probatum est. H.C.

For a Mad or Frantick person.

Take Mustard-seed contused in to Wine & tye it hotte to his head. it repelleth all forage & headacke. it causeth a man to rest & cleanseth ye braind.   H.C.

When a man falls into Madness,

Take Salt M. j. & rubb both hands & feet therewith. then take ye herbe Dipsacus & contused it well untill it be pappe & sue gently tye this to ye head of ye patient & when it is dry take fresh & lay thereon till such time as he begin to sleep.   H.C.

For ye Lunatick.

Take a Hedg-hogge & make broth of him, & lett ye patient eate of ye broth & flesh.

A cleansing Water for ye hands or face.

R. half a pound of Salt-peter of ye purest or whitest, half a pound of Tartar put them in a crusible such as ye melt gold or silver in, ye said Tartar being beat as small as ye said Peter, put a fyre-Coal to it & it will burn downe to ye bottom. when it is cold beat ye same into a gross powder again. put ye powder into a beast-bladder tye it close & steep it in fair water ye quantity of a pottle 6 houres, then lett it rune through Cap-paper (by way of filtering) put ye Water of ye finde ye bladder into a basin into some glass, & ye that is within ye bladder into some other glass & keep this for ye better. 2 spoonfuls will serve at a time to which ye may add a spoonfull of Rose-water.   H.C.

For ye Mother

R 2 ounces of ye powder of Bucke horn & put it into a quart of old Ale Boyle it from a quart to a pinte. drinck ye pinte at a draught 2 takinge will serve.   mrs Sheppe

For Deafness.

Take a great Oyster-shell & fill it with fasting spittle, lett it stand 2 dayes or 2 nights in a dunghill. then take it out & putt one drop in ye eare & stop it with black wooll so it is well likewise with ye same.   mrs...

An Oyle good for ache of bone or flesh.   Sr Alexander ... in his mares

R a handfull of Ciderage otherwise called Arsesmart & cut it small ye stalkes with ye leaves & put them into a glass of even portion of oyle olife. then stopp well ye glass & put it into Rotte horse dung, & let it be there ye space of 15 dayes. the take it out & strain it through a fine linnen cloath & ye oyle will rune through flesh or bone & fetch out ye ache clean. as hath been often proved.   H.C.

For ỹ longs-euill.

Take Collombine & stamp it & drinke ỹ iuice w̃ Wine, & it helpeth.
R. Groundsell ỹ leaues & flowers stamped w̃ a little Hogge-greafe, Saffro & Salt.
R. Archangell stampd w̃ Vineger & applyed in maner of a poultis.
R. ỹ leaues of Rue, pound the w̃ Swines-greafe & applye it.
R. Gote-greafe pounded w̃ Hogges-greafe.
R. Indian-pepper pounded & mingled w̃ Hony, & apply it.
R. Balme leaues stamped & mixed w̃ salt & vfe it.
(A Dagges tonguz stild & hony it about ỹ neck. — or w̃ stopping.)

H. C.

For ỹ k evill. kernells & Emerods.

R. ỹ root of Water Betony in ỹ end of somer, & after ỹ haue made them clean, stamp them w̃ fresh-Butter & put them into an earthen veffell close couered, set them in some moist place or dampish for ỹ space of 15 dayes & afterwards let it be melted, w̃ a soft fyre & strain it, & lay it vp to ỹ vfe.

For ỹ k.-Euill.

R. Folefoot stamped w̃ his rootes, ỹ flowre of ỹ seeds of Lyne or flax & ỹ greafe of a Barrow-Hogge, mixe them all together make thereof a plaster & lay it vpon ỹ soare chaunging it thrice a day, & all ỹ sores of ỹ difeafe will be refolued into sweat after they be healed wash often ỹ place w̃ White Wine by ỹ space of 10 or 15 dayes.

How to knowe ỹ k. euill.

R. a ground-worme aliue & lay him vpõ ỹ swelling or sore & couer him w̃ a leafe. If it be ỹ difeafe ỹ worme will change & turn into earth & if it be not he will remain whole as found.

H. C.

For pain in ỹ breast

R. clarifyed Hony & May-butter ana ℥4. Comen ℥i. Annifs-feeds ℥s Licoriza ℥s. mingle thefe together in maner of an Electuary, & vfe this fasting. for it is a principall medecine.

For one ỹ is sick after a full stomack.

R. fenell & chiu it in thy mouth. spitt out some & take down some it is a prefent remedy.

An eafy vomitt to cleanfe ỹ stomack.

R. ỹ iuice of Wallwort drink it w̃ white wine an egge full at once & it cleanfeth both vpward & downeward.

Against a Surfett. & difeafes thereof arifing.

R. ỹ flowres of Broome & still them, & drinel ỹ water morning & euening H. Henry ỹ 8 vfed this water for ỹ same.

H. C.

For a Cough of ẙ Lungs. or Consumptiõ.

℞ Syrop of Licoriza, Maydenhaire, Hisop & Harehound mixed together and supp thereof frõ ẙ end of a Licorize-stick bruised.

For fainting of Women.

℞ Ligni. aloes grated & type ẙ same in a clout. dipp ẙ same in cold Vineg & sue applye or hold it to ẙ nose.

For Cough of ẙ Lungs. & Consumption.

℞ Garden-Snailes nu. 5. break off ẙ shells of them; then boil them in a quart of new. milk of a redd-Cowe till it come to a pinte & a half. drink of this first & last & at all times of ẙ day.

To break an Impostume. in a mans body.

℞ Tansey a good handfall, & wash it in redd-Wine, & grinde it in a Mortar & wring out ẙ juice & drink out spoonfull every day & it will purge ẙ Disease downward without pain.

Against spitting of ẙ Lungs.

℞ Oyle of Oringes. or ẙ Syrop of Lemons is eaten helpeth.   Or
℞ Oyle of Oringes 3 i. & Capons-grease ℥ i. anoint ẙ stomach therto: & lay theron a Lamb skin dressed w̃ ẙ wolly-side next ẙ body, ẙ shirt between & chafe in ẙ oil against ẙ fire, & give him oyle of Vitroll in Plantin-water.   H. C.

A most p̃tious Balme or Oyle made by Matth: Lucatelly Ital.

℞ Venis-Turpentine unwashed of ẙ cleanest one pound, of ẙ best Sallet-Oyle 3 pintes & a ẙ of a pinte, of Bee-Wax half a pound. Sanders one ounce, & strong-Wine a pinte. / first slice ẙ wax very small & boyl it in a skellet over a soft fyre, & when it is throughly boyled, then putt in ẙ Turpentine, & when ẙ is throughly boyled, putt in ẙ Oyle & lett them all boyle a pretty while, & after putt in ẙ Sanders w̃ ẙ hand at 3 times still stirring it & lett ẙ boyl softly. still stirring them frõ ẙ begining till ẙ take them frõ ẙ fire. & when it is well boyled, you shall see it grow redd on ẙ sides of ẙ skellet— & ẙ must have a great care ẙ it boyl not over, for yf it take fyre it will endanger ẙ house. then lett it cool awhile & strain it before it be quite could. otherwise it will not runne.

ẙ Vertues. / first ẙ said Oyle is good to heal any wound either inward or outward being squirted in warm into ẙ wound being inward, & outward being applyed w̃ fine line of linnen, anoynting also those ẙ therabouts, it not onely takes away ẙ pain, but also keeps it from inflamation, & drawes forth also all broke bones or any other thing ẙ else might putrify or fester it. for ẙ ẙ braines or forwards
(as ẙ

(as ye Heart, gutts or Liuer) be not touched it will heal it in 4 or 5 times dressing
2. for y^t noe other thing be applyed therunto.   2. It also healeth any Burning
or Scalding. likewise it healeth any Bruise or Cutt being first anoynted wth y^e
said oile, or a piece of Linen cloth or Lint dipt in ye said oyle warmed & layd to
3. ye place it will heal it w^{th}out any scarr remaining.   3. It takes away any
paine or grief y^t might grow by reason of cold. moysture, Catarhe, or Aches in y^e
bones or Sinewes, first anoynting ye place for often wth ye said oyle heated, &
4. a warm cloath layd vpō it.   4. It helps ye Head-ache, onely anoynting ye temples
5. or nostrills therw^{th}.   5. It is good against ye winde Collick, or stich in ye side aplyed
therto warm wth wett clothes 4 mornings togeather, & every time a q^r of an ounce.
6. 6 It is good against Poyson, & helpeth a Surfett, taking an Ounce therof in a little
7. Sack warmed.   7. It helpeth ye Byting of a madd dogge or any other beast.   8. It is
8. good against ye Plague anointing onely ye nostrills & lipps therw^{th} in ye morning before y^e
9. party goe forth, for y^t day (by God's p^missio̅) hee need not fear ye Plague.   9 It also
10. healeth a Fistula or Vlcer, be it neuer soe deep in any p^t of ye body, being applyed as aboue
11. for a Cutt.   10. It is also good against Wormes or Canker, being vsed as ye Cutt, but it
will require a longer time to help thē.   11 It is very good for one infected wth ye plague
12. Measells or ye like, so it be phisickly taken in warm broth   a q^r of an Ounce, 4 mornings
togeather, or sweat vpō it, it also keeps one frō vermin.   12. It also helps Digestion
anoynting ye nable or stomack therw^{th} when ye party goeth to bedd. It will staunch any
bloud p^sently of a green wound, putting a plaster of Lint on it or tye it very hard
ye said Oyle or Balsome may be kept 20 years, & be much better for it.

                                                                            Mrs Thealeston.

            for weaknesse.

Take 4 spoonfulls of Plantain-water & putt to it half a spoonfull of y^e
powder of Swine's clawes.   Y^u must take ye clawes & wash them & cutt off
all ye haire frō thē, & dry them in an ouen & beat & sift them to as fine
a powder as y^u can. Let ye party y^t is weak vse this for 9 or 10 dayes, or
longer y^f occasion be, & keep her bedd y^f there be great occasiō, or otherwise
but 2 or 3 daies at ye first.   While shee is in this course
let her drinck (ye last after shee goeth to bedd) a draught of Ale mingled
wth Nutmegg & Suger.   /   this is an approoved medicine for Children
y^t canot hold their water   or women y^t haue ye Mother in any kinde
weakened.
                                                                            Mrs Bushell

For y Dropsye in y legges.

Seeth oates in water untill they be tender. then let y party diseased ... his legg y is swollen over y vessell y it may receive y fume or smoke of y said oates. & cover y party wth something y it may goe down round about y vessell & then blisters will come up^o y legge or swoln place out of wch will runne much water & corruptio̅. then after anoint the place wth butter. Doe thus 4 or 5 times yf need be.

/ y da: Sh... ... and
wth m^{rs} do: Hutton.

A gentle Purgatio̅ for a sick or weak body.

Take 20 good damask Prunes clean washed. then take half an ounce of Rubarb thinne sliced. stirre y prunes wth y Rubarb in faire water & damask Rofe water, wth a little Sugar. turne them oft & keep the close covered till they be very tender, then putt the̅ in a glass, & in y Morning eat 3 or 4 of the̅, & yf y please a spoonfull of y Syrop & fast an hower after.   in fra 172.   Sbid.

A Tysan.

Take Borage, Langdebeif, Sorrel, Endife Cinquefoil 2 handfulls of Barly well picked & both ends taken off. then take half a handfull of red-fennell rootes. a quantity of Liquorize, Sugar-candy. figges, dates, great Reisons.   Boyl all together fro̅ a gallo̅ to 3 pintes.   Sbid.

For a skald-Head.

Take Oyle-Olife & putt it into a dish of fairwater & beat or stirr the̅ well together as y would make butter. then take it upp. & putt it into a vessell, & putt powder of Brimston & May-butter thereto & make an oyntm^t thereof wherwth anoint y foare head & it heals it   Sbid.

To make one Sleep.

Take Camomil, Rye-bread. ... & Batony of y wood & grinde them well together. then wth Vinegar putt it into a panne, fry it well untill it be somewhat drye. then take a cloath & make a plaister & apply it Rote about y head, or y foles of y feet. strow vp̅o y hearbes y powder of Nutmeggs. & about dout hee shall sleep be hee never fo sick.   S...

For y Scabbs in child̅re̅.

Take Oyle of Rofes y weight of 6. m comon falt & a little fresh Butter stirred all together. untill it become an oyntm^t.   S...

A Restorative after weaknesse by a Lask

Take an old Red-Cock & boyl him till ye may pick out ye bones, then bruise thē & putt thē in again into ye broth if they weere soddē in, putt therto Marrow of an Oxe, & half an ounce of Quibbibes, half an ounce of Cloues, half an ounce of Nutmegs; & 3 penny weight of Saffron. make powder of all this & putt it to ye Cock & close it yt noe ayre come out, & when it is enough let him eat therof & sup ye broth. it restoreth.

Fd. ye La: Sheff.

For a child yt is weak or lame in her joynts. (In ye Rickets.

Take a great sort of Black Snales in May. chop them or stamp them small, & boyle them in May-butter or other butter a good while, then putt it in an earthen pott to keep it. When ye will vse it anoynt ye weake or lame joynts before ye fyer spred some of it on a cloath & bind it vpon ye place as hote as they can suffer it. vse it as long as yu need it.

Fd.

Rise-pottage good for a Flux.

Take al good hand full of Oken-Bark & boyle it in runing water a gallon to a pottle, or more, then strain it & let it coole. then take half a pound of Iordan Almonds, beat them in a mortar wth ye Bullet, & all on, after strein them wth the foresaid water, & foe wth Rize make rize Pottage. Likewise Rize may be beaten wth Almond-milk & foe it doth restore nature.

Fd.

Pro Hæmorrhusa.

Take Plantain-water a pinte. Gume-dragon a drāme, gume Arabicke as much. putt ye gumes into ye said water in a bottle-glafs, stirring or shaking it 9 dayes together. When ye vse it giue to ye woman 2 spoonfulls at a time (morne & eveening) & fast half an houre after.

D. Bush. McArwell

For ye Eyes, for to clear ye sight.

Take ye whites of 2 new-laid Egges & beat them in a pewther dish for 2 houres together till it stand in a tower. then let it stand 8 houres. then power out ye oile frō it. then take (Benwood, or Dafy rootes & leaues to=gether well washed & beat in a woodan dish wth a rowling pin & strein out ye juice. Then take 3 spoonfulls of ye oile of Egges, & 1 spoonfull of ye other juice, & 1 spoonfull of ye best english-Hony. Mingle them all together and strain them through a piece of new Holland-cloth & foe putt it vp in a glafs for ye vse. When yu are in bed at night putt one drop of it into either eye & foe sleep. & when yu awake in ye morning doe as much as yf yu can sleep after for twinke at least, half an houre & vse it 3 or 4 dayes together or longer as ye see cause.

D.E.D.B.

For y͛ stomack-Wormes.

Take Turmerack half an ounce. Long-Pepper a quarter of an ounce
beat them to powder. then take y͛ leaf of a swine 2 ounces & shred
it very small. then putt them all into a woodon dish, & 2 peny-worth
of Treacle with them. then beat them again w͛th a rowling-pinne and
till they be well mingled all together. then putt them in a little
square ~~bagge~~ (or somewhat long) folded vp & quilted. & applye it
to y͛ stomach 9 nights & dayes w͛thout stirring it.

D. B.

To make Trochisk for y͛ Rhume, or Cough of y͛ Lungs.

Take a quarter of an ounce of Enula campana-root, half an ounce of
Liquorice, half an ounce of Anice seeds, a quarter of a pound of Sugar-candy
or fine sugar, all finely beaten & searced. then beat it in a morter w͛th as
much gum-dragon steeped in rofe water as will binde it together. then work
it vp in little cakes or rowles, w͛th some of y͛ foresaid powder, & when they be
throughly dry. y͛ may keep one of u͛e in y͛ mouth as y͛ have occasion.

M͛. Moth.

y͛ La: North's receipt for makeing Juice of Liquorice.

First make a decoctio͛ w͛th Raisons of y͛ sunne, Anice seeds, Liquorice, Maidenhair, Colts-foot, figges, boyl all theise in 3 quarts of water, till half be con=
sumed. then take of choife Liquorice 1 pound & a half well scraped &
grosly bruised. then put it into y͛ decoctio͛ while it is scalding hott.
& foe let it remain for 24 howres. then strain it & prefs all y͛ liquor
as hard out as y͛ may. for y͛ Liquorice have noe juice therin. This
donne, boile it in a fair well leaded panne or skillett, stirring it
alwaies vntill it waxe thick. then take it fro͛ y͛ fire, on difhes in
small quantities, & foe lett it lye vntill it dry. then y͛ may make
it in balles, in what quantity y͛ please.

foe M͛. Mothers.

y͛ La: Bowis receipt for y͛ same. to be made in y͛ beginning of May.

Take 4 ounces of Liquorice scraped, beate & finely searced. 5 or 6 handfulls
of tender toppes of Hysope, 4 handfulls of foal-foot & hore-hound. a good hand:
full of Rofemary flowers, & a handfull of Maidenhair. stamp all theife to=
gether in a stone-Mortar, & strain them into a fair bafon, w͛th a pinte of Hy:
fope-water, or fair running-water. putt in y͛ Liquorice & boil it till it be
as thick as good cream, then strain it again through a fine strainer and
put it again on y͛ fire, & boyl it a good tyme stirring it continually till it
be very thick. then putt in 3 or 4 ounces of ~~red~~ Sugar-candy, & boyl it still

till ye may fee ye Bafon-bottom, stirring it still, then make it up in balls
or rolles at y^r pleafure, keep it allwayes nigh ye fyer. ye quantity of
a beafe will stopp ye blungone.

m^{rs} Matthews.

For nourishing a weak-body.

Take a pinte of Allegant, a good handfull of Raifons of ye funne, stone them
& beat them well in a mortar, & take ye Yolks of 2 Egges, mingle thes all
together & fett them on ye fyre, & when it is warm take a good quantity
thrife a day .

y La Vofula Vaughan

for a Purge.

Take an ounce of fena, a dragme of Mace, ginger, anifeeds liquorice
Coriander feeds & pulypode of ye oke of each a dragme being dryed & beat
then beat all theife together grosly & putt them into a pinte & a halfe
of old strong ale, then tofs them fro pott to pott half an howre, then
let it stand half an howre: this doe 3 times & foe let it stand
a day or a night then strain it, & putt to as much fugar as will
feafon it & foe much nuttmegge as you think good. Lett ye party
drinck ye one half at night when they goe to bedd, & ye other half
in ye morning at 7 of ye clocke, & 2 howres after take broth or fome
fuch thing as they like. This may be given to a Child, or old bodye
but if they be of a middle-age ye may put in 3 penny weight of
rubarb finely fliced, it must be putt into a piece of fine linnen
cloath & hang in ye forefaid stuffe, & foe lett it stand 2 or 3 howres
& now & then croush it till all ye strength of ye rubarb be out.

m^{rs} Matthews & m^r Egletly.

For a Could

Take halfe a pinte of white wine vineger
too ounczes of Aneseeds beaten.
too ounczes of sweet-fennell seed
one ounce off English Liquorice
boyle thes a quarter of an hower & strain itt from
ye liquor then putt too spoonfull of line or
virgin honye in a silver dish to a Sirrop.
Take a spoonfull when you goe to bedd, & so much
in ye mornings untill itt be speat

Sr Fer Fairfax

For ye Splene.

Take a quart of Claret & put into it half a pinte of Burrage-water.
a handfull of Balme, half a handfull of Rosemary topps & half a hand full
of Burrage wth flowers. 2 oranges wth some Cloues in them roasted very soft
in ye Embers, cutt them in ye middle & turing them in as hott as y^u can.
It must first be seasond wth sugar to ye liking. & hang therein a bagge
of Saffron.

Mrs. Elis: Chelmely.

To make one sleep.

Take a pinte of Cowslip-water; 2 ounces of conserue of red-rose, let y^m
steep 2 or 3 howres. then streyn it & put some 6 spoon fulls of syrop of
Gilly flowres, some 4 or 5 droppe of ye oyle of Vitriall. take some 6 spoonfulls when y^u goe to bed & it will make y^u sleep.

A water for to clense a sore troubled wth red humors or itching.

Take a pottle of smithy trough water stirre it up when y^u take it. then
boyl it & when it riseth take ye black scume off. then take a quarter
of a pound of roach Allome beat small & 3 spoonfulls of Honey, 2
good handfulls of great sage leaues, one of woodbin leaues, a little rosemary & a little Hysope. boyl all theise togeather a good while. then putt
it in a pott & keep it & warm a little of it & some of ye sage leaues
& bath ye soare therin. & when y^u haue layd salue on ye soare. then
spread all ye place as farre as any heat goeth & it helps wonderfully.

Mrs Carington.

An^o for ye same. a water &c

Take 3 q^{ts} of smithy water & let it boyle softly on a clear fyre
& as ye scume riseth take it off. when y^u haue soe done take it off ye fire
& put into it half an ounce of burnt Allom & as much White Copperas
then set it on ye fire & let it boyle 3 or 4 walmes. then let it be powred
into an earthen or pewther dish & let it stand all night. then put it
into stone bottles. when ye sore any soare wash ye soare first wth it
then take more fresh & dipp lint therin & lay it vpon ye soore. &
soe doe thrice a day till it be whole. / y^u must dipp cloathes 2 or 3
times double & lay vpon ye lint. / J. La. selbye.

A water for ye eyes.

Take seladine, fenell, sage Rosemary, Vervein & Rue of each one good-
handfull & wash them clean. then drye them again wth a linne cloath. then
putt them into a Limbeck & distill them & let ye patient drop some of
this water into his eyes often times & this will recouer his sight again
although it be supposed to be almost past recouery. / ye La: selbye

'73.

For ỹ Ricketts.

Take a pound of Currance, wash them well & boyle them in a gallon of spring-well-water till ỹ half be wasted, upon a clear fyer. then take them & strein them & putt thereto 12 spoonfulls of white-wine-vinager & put it into ỹ water-warme. & give them morne & night 6 spoonefulls at a time. or any time when they are thirstye.

Then 6 dayes after take a redd-Cocke about 2 yeares old & smother him in his blood & let him lye on ỹ ground about an hower. then dresse him & wash him clean & set him on ỹ fyer-to boyle in a clean pott off about 2 gallons of clear water & put thereto a handfull or 2 of Hearts-tongue, a handfull of Liverwort dressed clean & a Comfrey root or 2. a little handfull of Hysope & Time (more of Hysope then Time) a handfull of broad-Plantaine leaues. boyle all theise together with ỹ Cocke upo a soft fyer till ỹ Cocke fall in pieces & there be some 2 quarts of broath then take out ỹ cocke & hearbes, & bray them in a mortar bones & all. Strein them all together, then wash ỹ pott clean & putt ỹ broath in again. putt thereto half a pound of Reisons of ỹ sunne clean washt & putt thereto a pinte of redd wine a gill of English-honey. & 2 quarts of ỹ best Ale. Take half an ounce of Cinamon & bray it 2d worth of Saffron rubd. 4d worth of Mace, boyle all theise together for ỹ space of half an hower till it be boyled to 3 quarts & a half. Use this morning first & night last. & ỹ same being warme anoint ỹ back & joynts therewith. & keep them warme. & yf any thing be offensiue to ỹ stomack anoint ỹ joynts for much ỹ more.

ỹ La: Selbye.

For ỹ Yellow-Iandis.

Take a Buries-root ỹ greater ỹ better, scrape it cleer, then take a pott of newe Ale & putt ỹ roote therein & ỹ ale will boyle, & lett it be therein one day & one night well stopt. then lett ỹ patient drink one draught 2 or 3 times & he will be whole. certainly cured.

ỹ La: Widdrington.

A noble-receipt for ỹ Black-Iandis.

Take a gallon of Ale, a pinte of honey & 2 handfulls of redd nettles & take a penniworth or 2 of Saffron & boile it in ỹ ale (ỹ ale being first scumed) then boile ỹ honey & ỹ nettles therein all together & strain it well & drink every morning a good draught thereof for ỹ space of a fortnight. for in that space (god willing) it will cleare & perfectly cure ỹ black-Iandis.

ith. ỹ La: Widd:

148

A gentle purge for a weak body.

Take 20 good Prunes clean washed, & half an ounce of Rhubarb thinne sliced, stew them together in fair water wth a little Sugar. turn them oft & keep them close covered till they be very tender & in a morning eat 3 or 4 of them & yf y^u please a spoone full of ye Syrop. & fast an hower after. (Syr: &c.)   ye La: Widdrington.

A wine against Melancholy.

Take a pottle of White Wine, of Sage of Hierusale & Harts-tongue of either one a close hand full. Rosemary as much as of ye other then give all a boile on a soft fyre. then putt therin a pinte of Spring-well Water. & straine it after you think ye a pinte is spent in boyling of ye wine. Take a good bear-glasse full in ye morning, at 4 of ye clock (afternoon) & last at night.
                                                    Mrs Dor: Hutton.

The Chalybeat Wine. ag^t ye Skurvye, Iaundiss &c:

Take of White-Wine 1 pinte. of Chalybs prepared wth sulphur 1 ounce of Romun-Wormwood 1 pugill. trochiskes of Agrimony 2 drams. Species Hiera picra 1 dram. Infuse these in ye Wine close stopped for 2 daies, shakeing ye glass thrice or thrice a day. then
Take of garden Scurvigrass 6. handfulls. Water-cresses & Brooklim of each 4 handfulls. beat these well & press forth ye juice, wch being putt into a glass must be clarifyed by filling ye glass in warm water & runing it through a wollen-streiner. Take of these juices 3 spoonfulls, & 6 of ye Wine every morning. for 15 days.
Tho: bycause this quantity will serve onely for 5 days, & therfore
y^u must prepare y^t thrice.
                                           ye La: El: Belasis. glass

for - Phlegme or Fleame.

Take Betony & drye it & make powder of it & keep it till y^u need When y^u would use it take a quantity of Honey & of ye powder, & make 2 or 3 Pilles & swallow them downe last in bedd, & it will void ye phlegme.

for ye same.

Roast Onyons vnder-Roast embers & eat them wth Hony & Pepper & Butter morning & evening, in few dayes they shall feel ye brest loosed, & phlegme easily to be avoided.
                                                  ye La: Widdrington.

149

A Salue. to be made in May.

Take Valerian, Touesan, Scabious, Plantain, Ribgrass, Bramble & Woodbind-leaues, Agrimony, & Red sage of each an handfull. Lett them lye and wither upon a board untill y̌ next day. then shred them small & work them w̌th a pound of May-butter unwashed or salted. then put th̄ē into an earthen pott & bury them in y̌ ground 10 dayes. then put th̄ē into a panne & boyl them o̅n a soft fire, & when it is almost boyld putt in Bees-wax half a pound, Rozen a quarter of a pound, & some Turpentine into a part of it w̌ch you would haue to draw most.

y̌ La: Constable.

To purge y̌ Liuer for y̌ Scuruye &c

Take Rhubarb 2 ounces, Scuruygrass, Watercresses, horse-Radish & Dock-roots āna an handfull. hang theise in a bagge w̌ch in a gallō of ale & after 2 or 3 dayes drinck of it

m̄rs Hickringill.

For y̌ Jaundise.

Take Ale 3 pints saffron 2 worth. wormes a good handfull well washed & beaten in a mortar, strein them into y̌ ale, & w̌th 2 worth of Seney. & a little sugar drinck it

To make a Consumptiō-plaister.

Take Burgundy-pitch, Rozen Bee-wax of each a quantity 2 ounces & melt them together, then take a quantity of Turpentine & an ounce of y̌ oyle of Mace y̌ quantity of a gill melted altogether. then spread theise upō half a sheeps-skin. then take a Nutmegg grated & strow it thereon. The plaister is to be laid to y̌ spoone of y̌ Stomack & cutt to y̌ bredth of a hand

for the tooth-ach

Rx white arssnike and bole Armoniak of each a like quantitie, make these up into a small pellet with a drop of aqua-vitæ a drop of sallet oyle and a little lint, stop therewith the hollow of the grieued tooth 2 or 3 howres. swallow not but spit out the rheume that shall flow into the mouth and let not y̌ party sleep while it is in the mouth

yor w̄

VERE HARCOURT

Take Hartshorne rasped one ounce, Ginger
slyced one quarter of an ounce, Junoeberries one ounce
Figges halfe a pound, tow Oringes the rine and meate,
take Turmentall roots one ounce, Angellica roots one ounce
Angelica stalkes and leaues, Elder floures, Red bramble
buds and leaues, Red sage, Rue, and Sassafrige of stalkes and
leaues, of each of these herbes one handfull or champt all
theise in a Morter, put them to three pottles of white wine
and halfe a pinte of white wine vinger put all into a pott
and ruber it cloase, let it stand twelfe howers, then strane
it out with a presse that noe liquor remained in the herbes
put it into a bottle cloase stopped, It will keepe halfe a yeare,
itt as good when it is somer as at the frost day,
For preuention take tow spoonfull euery morning fasting and first
one hower after; it will make you haue a good stomacke to your
meat and not trouble you at worke; If anie haue taken ye
infection this will purge and vomitt till it hath wrought out ye
infection, if it make the partie sick giue them three spoonn=
fulls euery halfe hower till it worke noe more. It hath bene
knowne to worke in those that haue bene very much infected
tow dayes and a night very stronly

A water for the same.
If woomwood steept in the best white wine vinger, take
a spoonefull in the morning an hower before you eate;
tis very good to preuent infection.

A Direction against the Plage
Take three pintes of Malmesey and twell herbes Sage; and pue
of each one handfull and lett them all boyle together till
it come to a quart, then straine it and sett it on the fier
againe and put therto one pennieworth of long proper, halfe
an ounce of ginger, a quarter of an ounce of Nutmegs
all beaten together then lett it boyle alittle and put therto
fower pennieworth of Metridate, tow pennieworth of Treakell, and
a quarter of a pint of the best Angilica water, take it al=
wayes name breath morning and euening a spoonefull or tow
if you be alredie infected and sweat thereupon, if not
infected one spoonfull a day is sufficient, halfe a spoonfull
in the morning and halfe a spoon all at night, this is not only
good for the common plage but for the small pox Measels
purpots, and diuers other Soyensoye.

A Soveraine water of Dr Chambers phesitian of London. wherewith he did many Cures and kept the receit thereof secret till a little before his death, and then hee imparted it to Dr Abbott Arch Bishop of Canterbery

Take a Gallon of white wine I meane Gascoyne wine, then take Ginger, Mace Cloves Aniseeds fennill seeds. Carroway seeds and Gallingall, of each of theise a dram, then take Sage red mint rose leaves time and wild time rosemary camomill Lavender tops, and pellitory of Spaine of each of theise a handfull, then beat the spices small and the hearbes alsoe and putt them all into the wine and lett them stand 12 howers stirring it divers times Distill it in a Limbecke and keepe the first water by it selfe for it is the best, and the second is good too but not soe good as the first,

    The vertew of this water followeth

It Comforteth the vitall spirits, it helpeth the inward diseases that come of cold, it is good against the shaking of the palsey, it helpeth conception in women that be barren, it helpeth the wormes within the body, it helpeth the stone in the bladder it Comforteth the Stomacke ... the old Cough, it helpeth the tothrach; it ... the ... ..., it helpeth the stone in the raines of the backe it presently ... a stinking breath, and whosoever useth this sometimes and not often it preserveth them in the strenth of their bodies and shall make them seeme young long, it Comforteth nature marvailously.

If it stand in the son all sommer it is much the better A sponefull of it fasting once in 5 dayes: oftner if urgent occation call for it You may if you pleause ad of Cynnamont and nuttmegs a dramme of each

A Poultace for a Sore brest

Take of Stinking Hemlock, Gundgale, House Leeke, &
Lavender betts, of each a handfull, pound them
very small all together, put to them a hand
full of Rye meales, & a egge boyled hard, & 3 ounces
of Boores grease

For ye Stone
Take a little Castle soupe, & scrape it into posset drink made with
marsh Mallows roots and drinke it, & bath that part in Castion sope
For ye same by St J Gener
Take a pottle of milk, & slice sassafras into it, still it & drink of
that water.

To stay Griping in ye Belly
Take Charkcole & when its well burned in ye fier, take some of the
embers of it & put into a wooden dish, & when its well quenched with
Aqua vitæ, then apply it as hott as you can.

To cure Chilblanes
Take Bears suit & red rose water, & mix them together hott, & soe apply it
For Mullens Kernal for heat in ye face
Take ye powder of Flowselfor & Swines grease mixe them together, & soe apply it
For a Cough or Stoping with flegme
Take a pint of Red rose water, & ... of white suger candy & boyle that
into a surrop, & take now & then a spoonefull of it.
To strenthen ye back a receit of Dr Miers
Take a pint of Allagant & a large handfull of Raysons of sunn stoned, beat
them well in a mortr & that they may beat the better put to them
2 or 3 spoonefulls of white wine take ye yolke of 2 new lade eggs beat
them well, mix all together & straine them, this quantitie serves only
for trise or thrise & this you must take for 9 or 11 mornings together
fasting, drink it as hott as you can indure it, & fast one hower
after it.

Gravel

Jobs millipedes white Amber Anna. ℥ß
nutmeg ʒij Chio Turpintine as much as will
make them into a Mass which form into —
midling pills make Eight pills of a Dram
and take four at a time. P. Watson ————

Tooth ac ————

Crude Opium camphire ann grain putt ym —
into a bag & hold to yͤ Teath ————

Sacrum Saturni ℈ord Rub ℥ i. ℈ L Gill of Plantain
Water: allways Shake yͤ bottle when you —
used — ——

Raspb Curran Wine

To every peck of ripe Currants old, or 12 great quarts
measurd you
must putt 5 quarts of water, bruse ye berrys well
before you putt in ye Cold water putt ym into a tubb
with atappiat it, putt in apint of ale yest to 7 pecks
of Berrys. if you have not so many you may putt less
yest accordingly after you have stird it well cover
it with a Rugg or Blanckett and lett it stand till 2 days
& nights yn draw of ye Clear Juce at ye Tapp & to
every 4 quarts of Juce putt 1 lb of Sugr. at 6 or 7 daÿs
yn empty yor tub of ye Dregs. and turn in ye good into
ye tub again & lett it stand 2 days more ye same way
yn draw it of and putt into yr barrell & lett it
Stand till Aprill then bottle it this makes Strong
wine if you pleas you may putt a Little more water
to ye Dregs and make a small wine wth Ordinary
Sugr butt bottle it at 6 weeks End

Rasbery wine ye same way the Greeks
if you mix ye Raspps & Currance, a few quarts
of Rasps. will taste it- say apeck to ye above quanti

181.

To make the Plague or Surfeit water

Take of each of thes herbs halfe pound

		of Each of thes one pound
Dragons	wood Sorrell	
mugwort	feverfue	Rosemary
agrimony	Seabeous	Cowslip floors
Bettony	Cardus	Tormentill Root
Baum	Sage	
wormwood	Hearts ease	Each of thes halfe pound
Pimpernell	Tormentill	Elicampane Root
fumatary	Angelica	Butterbur Roots
Rue	wild time	
Celendine	Scordium	
Burnett	mary gold floors	
Spearmint	Red posy floors	
	Clove July floors	

Lett all thes above 3 or 4 dayes upon a table before
you use y'm & shred y'm very Small then putt y'm into
any Convenient thing as a large cream pott or
Kettle adeing to them as followeth ————

Each Sweet fenell Seeds
an Caroway Seeds
noe Cardimum well bruisd
Cloves
Natmeg Cinemon
Venice Treeckle
Diascordium
of Each Ounce

To all these add 3 Gallons of good brandy
and lett them stand to Infuse 4 dayes
Stiring y'm once a day & keeping y'e pott covered
then Still y'm in a Cold Stee keeping it
cool with wett cloths when the Surfeit
water begins to grow Sower taking
more you may boile Some of y'e Smallest
water to fine Sug'r & Litle amber Greafe
to a Syrup to Sweeten y'e Rest

156

Syrup of Clove July Floors ·————

Take half pound of Floors. put y'm into a pott.
& power 9 Gills of Boyling water upon y'm cover it
& Lett it Stand 3 or 4 houris then Strain it through
a seive & put two pound of Loaf Sug: to one pint·
& Give a boill or two & Scum it very well————
you may clear it up w'th whites of Eggs

Excelent water for horse & Eye or mans Eye
yᵉ wett. Rather strong for mans ———

Camphire soz: fine ora toll Bole Armeniack
4 ounce Blew Vitrioll: 4 ounce Lᵗᵗᵉ Burn Alloes.
in powder: putt it into 5 quarts: of Boyling water
& Lett it stand till its cold, putt off as much as
is Clear into any pott or Bottle for yᵉ Ey, & reserve
yᵉ other for any Sore or Brack Leall ————
you may if you please add to yᵉ rest of yᵉ Ingredients.
Saccum Saturni one aunce wᵗᵉ é Gill Plantain water
allway shake yᵉ Bottle when you Use it

Minced Pyes ~~the best way~~ —————

Take 13 eggs hard boyl'd through out half ye White
1/2 pd Suet 1/2 pd prunes 1/2 pd 1/2 Raisons Gill Sack quarter
pd Lemon peale 1/2 oz: of Cinimon & Nutmeg
Suger to yr taste Little mace & cloves 4 Apples
Shred all small & putt in alittle Verjuice for
Sharping & putt ym into ye Paes *see ye next page*

for an Ague —————

Take Jesuits ~~or~~ bark in fine Powder.
one ounce Salt of steel or Common ————
Green Copperas, quarter of an ounce ————
Jemmica Peper quarter of an ounce
Molloses ——— four ounces —
Mix those all together and take about the
quantity of nutmeg three times a day
when the fitt is not on —————

For An Ague

Take Clean Spiderweb half a drachm and Swallow 1 down.
in any form, for severall mornings Successively, when the
fit is off ; Six drachms of Barh aspoonfull of pepper & a nutmeg
mint up is Rum or [?] wind take bigness of a Nut every 4 hours.
probatum

185.   well shred ———— or 16 yolk & a lytle of say
1 pd Common Tripes; or 13 Eggs hard boyl. take half
the whites out ———— 2 pd Suet shred as small as
posible.——1 pd Raison 2 pd Prunes Ston'd well shred
1 pd Currants a nuts: to oz Sinemon to oz mac
to oz Cloves: 8. Sour aples. well shred gill ver
Juce gill Sack little brandy Sweten them
w sug'r to y'r taste ½ pd Cetron Peell ————————
best Recp for minced Pyes ————————

The Green Oyntment w'h is very good
for old Sores or Green Wounds La Cart Recet —
Sake of S't Johns wort Valerian Yarrow
Bugle Plantain Sanickle fox Gloves bettany
        ladymantle & yarrow
Croswort Soap wort ^ of Each of those herbs one
hand full. bruise the herbs well w'th two pound
of may Butter one pd of oyl Olive, Set it
in a Celler for ten days then boyl y'm an hour
over a slow fire and Straine out the herbs
add to the Oyntment Venice Turpintine half
a pound, bees wax one p'. resin'd rosen 2 pound
Verdegrease in powd'r. 2 drams resolve y'm alltoge'r
over a slow fire and Strain y'm again and keep.
for life in a well Glaz'd Earthen Pott ————
                    often Proved

160

146 The Strengthing Plaster —

Contra Rapturium ℥ ounce.
Seratum Santalinum &
oyntm: unguent Comitsse } 2 ounce. Each.
oyl mirtile Berry ——— 2 ounce.
powder of Mastick ℈.
Dragons Blood ———
Armoncalk } 3 drams Each
Biftort roots. & Galls
Red corrall yellow amber — 2½ D: Each.
Nutmeg ——————— 2 D

very good to lay on ye Back to prevent
miscariage or other Straines

Very Good Bitter wᶜʰ hᵃˢ Curᵈ Severall
in Agues when ye Bark Failed ———

Snake root ——— 3 ℈ᵖᵗʰ   put in to 4 gᵗ
Gentian ——— 2   of ale
pd: Hiera Picca — 3
   Camomile Floors. 1
   Safron ——— 3
   Swell Orange &
   Juneper Berry 1
        14 pence —

161

To Recover Drink when flatt or rather
turnd Sower ————
Take 3 quarts: spring water boyl it with
two pound of Brown Sugr and when
almost cool put a little yeast to it ————
when you Bottle your drink put into your
Bottle ye ⅛ of a pint, if yr ale be very flat
if not quite flat put in less — it will be
fit to Drink in 3 or 4 days.

Miles Robinson

187

The Balm–drops. Excellent for a Wound   £. 18.ẞ

Balsam of Peru one ounce: 2 : "
Storax Calamitar two ounces.   1 . 4
Benjamin *impregnated is Sweet Oyl.* — three ounces .... 2 : 6.
Spirit Wine two pounds...   1 . 8
Sucotrine aloes half an ounce — 4.
Myrrh D.° ———— ———— .. 4
Olibanum D.° ———— ———— ———— 2.
Angelica root. D.° ———— — — 1
S.t Johns Wort; *Flowers* D.°   ———— 1ẞ
~~Frankincense D.° the Charge Tot.~~   8 : 6

Put all these together into
a Bottle close stopt and let it Stand
in y.e Sun Six Weeks in the hottest
time O the year: then strain it —
through a fine linnen Cloth and put
it into Smal Bottles. Put the Dregs back
into the Bottle and fill it w.th Verjuce.
and keep it for Sprains or Bruises.
" in " men or "Horses ———
                    Eng.s further.

163

Neaver heat the Drops but apply it
cold It's good for any Wound
cut, Stab Shot. or Bite. it will Cure
the deepest wound in afew days. if rightly
made, and apply wth afeather, or drop in
If. the Wound has b^e^ndres'd wth any other
Remedy, be sure to wash it Clean
wth Wine or Brandy made hot, before
you apply ye drops, It will not-cure
So well as if no other thing had been
use, no plaster must be us'd wth it,
when a Wound is large its proper to
wrap it in a Clean Cloth to keep out Air
Its. alsoe good for a horse prick in
the foot or any other wound or Gall

Its alsoe a good remedy for the Cholick
or Flux, twenty or thirty drops taken
in Broth or a glass of wine
always keep y^r bottles closs stop^t ——————
have tried it wth good Success for Wound &
Robt Green

The Composition for the Gout 1690
Take an Earthen Vess.l that will
hold twenty Gallons fill it w.th
Elder Flowers full Blown and clean
pic.t, they will waiste considerably
therefor Continue to fill it up —
as long as you can y.t Flowers —
then put in two pound of Bay
Salt, one Gallon & half of any
sort of Vineger stir it well w.th
a stick and Corke it up close ———
and Set itr in the Sun for two Months
then Stirr it again and corke it as
before and Sett it into a Celler ———
keep it from frost and Stirr it once
in two Months for y.e first year ——
if it grows dry put in a little Vineger
if worms get in to it add a handfull of Salt —
It must be apply.d when the gout is near
the height and must be laid on fresh every
night and Morning ——— Probatum ———

165

a Reet for makeing — Daffys Elexer

Annaseed — 1 oz

Fennel seed — 1 oz gr. — 2

Span liquorice 1 oz half — 1

Rubarb — — 2 drams 1 : 3

Ellicampane 1 oz gr. — — 1

Manna — 1 oz half 1 : "

Jallop . 2 oz — . 1 . 4

Senna — + oz gr. . " 5

Saffron — half dram . " . 4

Raisons of the Sun half pound .3

Slice the liquorice

Stone the Raisones

Bruise the Jallop.

Tot Charge
4 : 11

Infuse those Ingredients for Six days
in two quarts of the Best Brandy
then Strain it out — Take two Spoonsfull
over night and the like in the morning

To make Shrub or *other bat* 192

Take Brandy six Gallons, put to it
the Iuce & rind of ten dozen of Lemmons
(or otherwise half Orranges) be Carefull
not to put in ye Seed or white part
othe skins, ad four gallons of Choice
white wine, and twelve pound of
double refind Suggar; put all together
into a Cask, and let it stand a month
or till it be fine, if its made of oranges only
twelve dozen is the quantity

To make Blacking for Shoos or boots

3/4 pd Bees wax
1 pd. best Soft soap or Sweet soap
1/16 barrel of lamps black
1 oz Gun powdr. Do Gum Arabick; beat & seared very fine
Dissolve the wax first, then add the Soap.
and melt it down likewise, then put in
the black and Gun powder, and let it
Boyl till it is tollerable Stiff but very slowly
Take it out othe pan, and work it very well
upon a stone or bord till you roll it up for use
observe to Soap yr hand. and yr place where
its wrought to hinder its Sticking

167

St Johnsworth Drops   Mrs Lydall '92

Take white wine one quart oyl olive
4 pound oyl Turpintine 2 pound
the leaves flowers and Seeds of St Johnswort
Each two large handfulls gently bruis:d
put all together into a greatt Glass Jarr po.
& Expose it to the Sun ten days
then Boyl them in the Same Expurg:d in
in a pot of hot water for ten howrs
put hay in along wth ye Jarr to keep
it fast Strain out the liqr and renew
the like quantity of the Herb ingreedien
boyl it as before and strain it again
and keep it for use

a Cheuse reet for a Cold by Dr Mead
Oyl of Sweet Almonds ___ 2 oz
Diacodion, Balsamick Swrup
and Aqua Mirabilis Each ___ } 1 oz
mix

To make Bramble berry wine 194

To every quart of berries put a quart
of water. squeese the berries and put pulp
& juice into y.e water, let it stand
all night. then run y.e liquor through
a bag or Cloth and to every six Gallons
off liq.r put 14 pound of Sug.r at 6.d
Stir it well and put it in Cask without
Yest let it stand ab.t 2: 3: or 4 months
to purifie then bottle it ~~rather over sweet~~ I have made by this rec.t

A Receipt for the Cure of a bite by
a mad dog. published by Doct.r Mead
Take. One dram of Ash Col Coloured Liverwort
One dram of Common peper in a pint
of Warm Milk, repeat this for nine or 12
Mornings Successively useing a Cold bath
at the Same time

169

For Rheumy Ey's where they are attend with a Flux of humours _____

Tincture of Hellabore three Ounces
Tincture of Cantharadies One Ounce
Spirit of Lavender } Each half an Ounce
Tinctr of Castor

Mix and give a Spoonfull in a glass of
Water and take it twice a day ___ If the
Superfluous humours can be wrought off
by Operations by Stool this will probably
carry of yr disorder by Urine _____

as three to five
Mix double quantity of Irrimston to
Allum Burnt, with Sallet oyl or any
other softning thing, give flowr of brimston
inwardly for three ch four Mornings
before yth rub. Two or three Rubbings
cure ye most inveterate veeh. _____
(ie) 3oz brimston } _____ Mrs. Johnson
2oz Allum __ }

An Exelent Eye Water. W.J. Lodg.
Take 1 Ounce of Hepatich Aloes in pocoder, Do white
Sug Candy, Ditto Lapis Tutty, prepared, half an
Ounce of Camphor finely shred Steep the Tutty
in breastmilk and change it every 3 or 4 hours
Then wash off the Milk wth a little Rose water and
put the ingredients into a Quart Sherry wine or Rhenish
I suppose steeving the Tutty in brest milk is to abate its strength

To Make German Black-ball for Shoes &c

Take 8 ounces of beeswax cut it small and put it into a pan to melt then put in 2 ounces of rendered mutton suet and put it to the wax and melt them together, Then take 6 ounces of Ivory black powder it in a morter and sift it through a hair sive and put it to the Wax & tallow and let them boyl gently together keep stirring all the while with a knife Then put in half an Ounce of Oyl turpintine when they are thoroughly mixed, Take a little soft sope and watch and rub upon a smooth stone or board, then pour down yͤ mixture and before its cold work it up with yͤ hands into rolls first rubing yͤ hands with a little sope to hinder its sticking ——

Liquid Blacking ——

To a pint of small beer put 1½ oz of Ivory black 1 oz of Gum Arabick & 1 oz of Sumach

171

Currant & Rasp. Wine best way
Take forty six quarts of Currts
rasps when ripe bruise and squeese
them through a Corn sieve Rinse
with a little water to make the pulp
pass freeler – add six quarts of Wrt.
put it into an Open tub with a tap
put in three spoonfulls of good Yest
Stirr well, & cover it up for 24 hours
draugh it of as Clear as you can
or run it through a hair sive   To every
Gallᵒ of Juice put 3 pounds of Lours
Lump Sugᵣ Then bury it into a lose Cask
wᶜʰ let be full or thereabouts. put in an
Oz. of Isinglass, let it Stand till Spring
and bottle it ———————   you may put
in Rasps to yᵣ likeing as 6 8 or 10 quarts
of yᵉ above quantitty ——————————

172

~~To make Chocolate Creams~~

~~the manner of Ch...~~

A Cure for ye bite of Mad dog Published
for ye benefit of mankind — In the News
papers in 1741 by a person of note —
Take 2 quarts of strong ale or wine Red Sage
and Rue of each an handfull and an half
Twelve cloves of Garlick bruised, — of Tin
and pewter scraped two spoonfulls —
of London treakle, or Venice treakle
one ounce, — Boyl these close covered till
half be consumed stir in the treakle when
the rest is boyled — pour it into bottles, Cork it
close, and it will keep a year, give three
spoonfuls morning and Evening, and a pint
is Sufficient for man or beast — Garlick
Rue and Salt, pounded together may be
apply'd to ye Wound —————

NB: This Medicine has stood a tryal
of 50 years Experience and was
never known to fail —————

See Folio 205

A Glister for the Stone — — — —

Take a knockell of vele or some other boni pese that 3 pintes of
water will couer it, scime it well, then put in 3 ounces of
rasens of the sonne & stones pecked out, and a god pese of
marchmalo root, scraped and pecked slised in then peces,
boyle thes in a pipken, vntell the mete will falle firme
the bones, then put in a lettell whole mace and halfe a spoon=
full of annesedes well beten, and let them boyle a lettell
while, then crush and bruse all to-gether and strane out
the broth, take allmost a pint of it and make it
sumething too salt to be eten and put in tow ounces of
course suger and 8 pence, or 12 pence of oyell of violettes
Let this be your glister although you should be neuer
so wele, if you nede it

in sommer in the place of marchmallo rotes
you may take a hanfull of malle leues and violet leues.

A neuer failing midisine for the bites of a mad dog taken
out of the Gentlmans Magazines for Oct.r 1746 ——
Take Rue Plantin leues Bonen Garlich Venis
treacle Mithridate and pewter scrapinge Each
4 ounces boyl all these ouer a slow fire in two qts.
of strong ale till one pint be consumed put it
into a bottle close stoped, and give nine spoonfulls
seuen mornings together to a man & thri to a dog

06 To Boyl Garn very white &
as I have Softten tryd ⸻

First put of a peck of Bran into
so much water as yͭ think will Cover
8ͭ 30 score of fine Garn (let it steep
ay 42 or 36 Hours)
2 nights in the water after it is
draind of through a course (Cloth) then
dry it — when quite dry prepare
2 oz of pot Ashes & 1 oz of Sweet sope
to Every pound of Garn — lay yͬ
pot Ashes into a qͭ or 2 of hott water
to dissolve — Then take yͬ sope and
rais e a lather with Clear soft water
wͨʰ put into yͬ kettle, and when
its almost ready to boyl put in yͬ pot
ashes & yͬ garn wͨʰ let boyl an hour
then yͤ take it out be sure to have a tub
of cold water to drop it into or yͤ heat
will tender it & spoile it Carry yͭ it away

175

and Ringe it well then mek a lather [20]
of Sope and wash it through again
a little Rock allum put into yͤ kettle
when its boyling – helps to festen yͤ gͦ

A Reciepe for a pottatoe pudding
Take a pound of pottatoes boyͩ & peel y
or either rofsted
Then beat them well. Take 6 Eggs —
& beat them and strain them throught
a hair Sive. then put yͫ to the potatoe
and mix them well together, add One
Nutmeg, & sugͬ. to yͬ taste; Dish it
up. abͭ. half an hour will bake it —
The potatoes must be cold before yͤ beat,
or they will lump —— D s. yͧ may add
a little melted butter if yͧ please. ——

208   for a tickling Cough

Take honey and Liquorise root Each 4oz
Flowers of benjamin &opium Each a dram
Camphire two Scruples, Oyl of Anniseed
half adram, Salt of Tarter one Ounce
Spt of wine rectified one quart ___
Digest the above in a covered Vessel for a
fortnight sheking it offten then decant
it for use ___ The doze for grown persons
from 20 to 100 drops for Children from
5 to 20 in white wine or Hysop water
Tis a good pectoral and admirably allays the
tickling wch provokes freqt Coughing it Opens
the brest and gives more liberty of breething
It deterges and Cleanses ye vinall glands and maks
way for their discharges it Rarifies & thins
the Viscid Cohesions of the Vessels and fitts ym
for Circulation & Secretion _____

Minced pyes   by Billy Hoppers Recet —

half a pound of Suet shred small One pound of Apples
full weight when cored   three q:rs pound of Currants ——
half a pound of Sug:r ~ quarter pound h:f Orange Lemmon & Citron
a little Cinnamon & ½ Gill of Gooseberry wine . ———

Rich:d Dunns Reciepe for to cure the bites of a Mad dog
Take one handfull of balm boyl it slowly in five gills of milk
till a pint be wasted Then put in the under mentioned
powders. when it is blood warm, and to a beast or horse
put in about a spoonfull, and for a dog swine or sheep
a knife point full, & the like quantity for a man, only
boyl it in water and add the powders when cold and let
them drink the quantity in two days and repeat it
for a fortnight or longer & bleed often bleed a hors. or beast
in the roof of y:r mouth and rub some salt on
the gum..

Camphire, Fenugrick, Turmirack, Longpepper, Grains
Bayberrys Aniseeds. Cummingseeds. Liquorice powder
Best bole and ground Ash koulured Liverwort, Each.
an ounce wele beet of, mix them all together and keep for use

10　　　　To Pickle Walnuts See another recipe in the other
book page 68 — — — — — —
Gather your Walnuts when a pin will pass through
them pretty easy — put them into a deep pot & cover
them over w Ordinary Vineg'r & Water, change them
into fresh every fourth day till abt 6 weeks are
past Then take 1 gallon of yr best Vineg'r & put therein
3 oz of Dill, Carraway, & Coriander Seed Each; grosly
bruis'd, Race Ginger 1 & ½ ounces Mace 1 ounce
Give it a boyl over the fire and pour upon your
Walnuts Also do for several times as you shall see cause
or cover the top w White mustard Seeds & a little
salt — Mind to keep them over head in the pickle

Major Davison Receipe for the Jaundice
Poke Fancey, Dandelion, Ground Ivy & Celandine
Each an Handfull beat them in a wooden bowl or
Morter and strain out the juice put to it a quart of
Ale and as much of yr inner rind of Barberry bark
as you can take up twixt yr two fingers & thumb. Infuse
the ingredients in the alf for 3 or 4 days then drink
½ a pint morning & night ——————

179

The Marquess of Granbys Recipe for Brewing
Small beer

One Bushell of malt — One peck of Wheat.
One peck of Oats; the Oats should be dryed so
as to grind with the malt & — Wheat, Brew them
with One pound of Hopps.
as you do other liquor, tap it at about
three weeks or a month old, and if fine bottle
it, this will make half a hogshead

To Refine Cyder
put two ounces of Burnt Allum to an hogshead

Orange ale
after ye ale is Turned into the Casks putt to Every
Anchor (and so in proportion) Two dozen Oranges
cut into quarters, and put into the Cask just as
they are cut

A Cure for the Stone in the Bladder—

Take Every day in any form that is most agreeable to the patient
One ounce of Alicant Soap, the internal part of it, wch is usually
of a blue colour, marbled with white, And drink three —
English pints or more—of Oyster or Cockle shell Lime
water, The Soap may be divided into three full doses,
the largest to be taken in the morning fasting. The
2d at Eleven O'Clock, and the 3d at 5 in the afternoon,—
drinking after each dove, a large draught of the Lime
water, and may at any time drink the Lime water after
dinr, or Supper, instead of other Liquor, The taste of
the Lime water may be blunted by adding a little milk to
it, and may be quite destroy'd by washing ones mouth
with little Vinegar & Water, Which however must be
immediately spit out again, but if the patient can't
take the Soap in this form, let him dissolve an
ounce in three gills of Lime water made warm,
and take this at three different times, drinking the rest
of the lime Water by it Self, The soap is not only proper
to be applied wth this shell Lime water, as it is endow'd
with great power in dissolving the stone, but as it prevents
costiveness, that might otherwise be occasioned by ye lime water,
But if any person afflict'd have an invincible Aversion
to Soap in any shape, The Drs Experiments give us reason

to think that Oyster & Cockle shell Limewater, drunk alone
in large quantities, will have greater Effect in dissolving
the Calculus, So if in the place of all Mrs Stephens
medicines, wch to many delicate people, can be of little use,
we may Sub-
stitute this Limewater wth Equall may probably with
greater ～～ Success

Abstain from all Acid & fermented Liquors as Vinegar
Wine, ale, Beer, Cyder, &c, for his Drink let the patient
take Water & milk, or a ptisan made wth pardey root,
of Marshmallows, & Liquorice, But if he cant confine
himself from some generous light, he may be allowed
now & then a little ～ small punch wth out Souring, It will also
be proper to be sparing in the use of Saltmeats, and
Honey, and to abstain from all fruits that have any
Acidity or sharpness, While on the other hand milk,
Sugar and animall food, Peas, Artichokes, asparagus,
Parsley, Turnips, Carrots, pottatoes, Radishes, Greenpease,
but particularly Onions, Leeks, & Callery may be freely
used. As the Cure depends upon the Urine's being
strongly impregnated with the Virtues of the Limewater,
the patient ought to drink no more of any other
Liquor—then is absolutely necessary to Quench thirst,

Turn over—

St

182

It may be observed by the Bye, that such as
have no stone in the Bladder but are subject to
to fresh fits of the gravel in the Kidneys, might very
probably prevent these by drinking every morning
Two or three hours before breakfast, a pint of Oyster
shell Lime water, Which though too small a quantity
to dissolve a stone, yet might possibly hinder any
new concretions, —————— If the Lime Water
should Occasion Costiveness it will be proper now
and then, to take a gentle purge of Aloes, Rhubarb,
Senna or Manna.————— The Oyster or Cockle shells for
making of water must lye long, exposed to the weather before
calcination, and when calcined, be perfectly white, and
used fresh from the fire, Seven, or at most Eight pounds
of boiling water, is to be poured upon one pound of y shells;
w.t boiling water gives a sweeter and softer taste than cold,
tho the Dissolving power of both is the same, but whether hot,
or cold, it should be allowed to stand 4 or 5 hours on the
lime, then decant it off, and filter it thro a cap paper,—
this water will keep for any time without attention, if closely
stopt up in bottles, but looses some of its qualities by
boyling, and the Surest Test of its goodness is, its changing
Syrup of Violets to a green Colour ————————

183

To Make poppy Surfeit Water —

To two gallons of Brandy put a peck of the
leaves of poppies one ounce of Sweet Fen'ad
half an ounce of Carraway Ditto Corriander eds
Two ounces of Liquorish sliced half pound of
good raison of the Sun stoned half a pound
of choice Figgs sliced half an ounce of Mace
D° nuttmeg D° Saffron bruise the Nutts
& pull to pieces the Saffron. Then mix all
these amongst the poppey & brandy & let
it Stand a month or Six weeks stirring
it Every day then run it through a course
Linnen bag — This I had from M.rs Buxton
as a Super Exelent Remidy ag.st Colick
pains but I shall add a quarter of a pound
of the Flowers of S.t Johns wort to y.e Composs.n

216

A Receipe for the Cholick sent me by J P

Scrape fine chalk and power a pint of soft
water upon Two spoonfulls of it, and pass
it through a Sive two or three times to
take off the grit Sweeten to yr taste
and drink it when you are attack't.
You must Stir it about or the
Chalk will Settle The water may either
be Hot or Cold when you put it to the Chalk
it is a Certain Remedy where the disorder
proceeds from Acidity in the Stomach
or Guts. ———————— I have try'd it with
great Success signed J Parton

A Recipe for making Mead

To Two stone of Honey put thirteen Gallons of warm
water stir it till the Honey is desolved Boyl in it
a bunch of Sweet marjoram, Balm, Rosemary
& Sweet Brriar, and put in Ginger & Cinnemon
Each a quarter of an Ounce, half an ounce of
Cloves; two Nutmegs Corriander Seeds & Carraway seed
Each an Ounce, Bruise the Spices & Seeds and tye
them up in a thin Bagg with a stone to sink it:
Let it Boyl an hour takeing of the Skim clean
off as it riseth. And when taken of the fire
put in the peals of Six Lemons and squeese in
their juices Work it with yest And when you Tunn
it leave out the Herbs & Spices — put into the cask
when you judge its done working half an ounce
of Isinglass desolv in a little of the Liquore
Bottle it at 14 days End ———————

Mrs Husley's famous Glister for Worms.
Take Rue & Lavender & Cotton Each three sprigs —
Anniseeds & Wormseeds Each. one Spoonfull
bruise & boyl them in a pint of Milk till —
a third is Konsumed then Strain it and Add
as much Aloes finely powd as will lye
on Sixpence & a little Treakle administer
it warm three or four mornings Successivly

    Andersons Pills ———

Take Juniper Berries, Senna, Burdock seeds, Coriander seeds,
parsley seeds, Carroseeds, sweet Fennel seeds, Liquorice Root,
Gentian Spanish Angelica root, Anniseeds Each one drachm
Cardus three tops, Boyl the above in half a pint of soft Water
to a quarter of a pint then strain the liquor and Add —
Barbadoes Alloes a quarter of a pound Christal Mineral
a quarter of an Ounce and Saffron one dram ——
Boil altogether very gently to the consistence of pills

To Pickle Lillo or Indian Pickle — 219.

Take of ginger 1lb let it lye in Salt and Water all
night Scrape it and cut it into thin Slices ...
it into a pot with dry Salt so let it remain till y
rest of the ingredients be Ready — Then take Garlic
1lb peal of the Skin & Salt it three days then we s...
it in Water and salt it again & let it stand
three days longer wash again and put it into
a Sive to dfrain and dry it in the Sun
Take Cabbage cut them in quarters salt them and
dry them in the Sun so do Colliflower & Cellery

Raddishes may be done the same way. only
Scrape them and leave on the tender tops, The
Water must be squeezed out of the Cabbage
French beans and Asparagus must be boild
two days only. after w they must have a boyl in
Salt and Water and then be drained in yd Sun
Take long pepper Salt it and dry it and white
Mustard seeds bruised Turmerick very fine put all
these ingredients into an Earthen Jar and put to
it a Gallon of Vinegar fill the Jar 3 qts full and if...
to it as you see Ocasion pr a fortnight — After this ti...
meet: so you may order Cucumbers, Samphire, Mustr...
plumbs or any other thing you chuse to have pickled
NB you are not to boyl any of these Save french beans on...
Asparagus or such things as must of Course be boyld or scalded

188

Lady Hodgsons Eye Water 220

1 ounce of Aloes Sucotrine   2 oz of Balsam of Tolu
2 oz of Storax   1 oz of White Sugr candy in powdr
1 oz of Tutty prepared
2 oz of Camphor shred very fine

Steep the Lapis Tutty in Brestmilk for 9 hours
changeing it every 3 hours then wash of the Milk
with Rose or Fennell water then put the ingredients
into a quart of Sherry Sack or strong white Wine
shake the Bottle 3 or 4 times a day for 10 days.

Mr Halls mixture for a Sprain or Bruise
Take two Ounces of Salt Petre or Nitre put it into
a pint of best Wine Vinegr add 2 spoonfulls of
Spirit of Turpintine & 2 spoonfulls of Spt. of Wine
shake the Bottle when you use it If it can be apply
before any swelling rise on the part it will do better

189

Two Specifics for the Stone & Gravel from
Treatise on those Disorders just published &
magazine for Aprill 1766

Take 8 Ounces of Pot-ash and 4 Ounces of q.
Lilm mix and put them together into a glass
then pour upon them a quart of boiling Soft
let the infusion remain twenty four hours
and then and afterwards filtrate it for use

Dr Chittchs Secret for the cure of the Stone
Take One Tea spoonfull of the strongest Sol
in two table spoonfulls of sweet Milk at
Breakfast and at going to bed; Before you
take a cup of of pure Milk, and immediate
swallowed the Medicine take another = &,
agrees with you for two or three days
—————— half as much more to the
The Author adds that the Genuine Recipe u
Genl Dunbar wch is the Medicine made us
who pretended to be the only Person who had

Take One Tea spoon full of the stronge.
in two table spoonfulls of sweet Milk a
Breakfast and at going to bed before yo
take a sup of pure Milk and immediat
if you find this agrees wth You for two o
add half as much more to the dose havi
owr author bro? the Valuable secret to lig
the hands of the low as well as the great that b
to be of the greatest Efficacy against the most pai
Share the satisfaction of contributing something to t

190

rise ——————

well with stale Urine to which add a

Hartshorn or crude Sal armoniack in

by it by way of Poultice

Another

ome Sal. armoniac in a little urine &

re dip a rag in it warmed and apply it

renewing it as need be ——

of all the Salts there are none more agreeable

and more penetrating than Sal Armoniac

extravasated blood for an Admirable man.

To Stop Vomiting ——

a spoonfull of Quincey's bitter Stomach Tinct.

Syrup of Oranges or Quinces it is

that bitters Sweetened are of great

stopping Vomiting when many other

been try in vain Another for the same

uce of a Lemon into a large Cup and mix with

much Salt of Tartar as will render it insipid

full and repeat till the Vomiting ceases if during

so much the better the same Mixture ——

imple Cinnamon Water or fountain and taken

ources is good for Fevers —— ....

191

To quench Thirst where drink is improp.
pour Vineg.r into the palm of the hand and snuf
the Nostrils and wash the Mouth with the same 'tis
ceiveable how much it will allay Thirst

For the Hiccough

Drop a single drop of Oil of Cinnamon on a lump of
refined Sug.r let it dissolve in the Mouth leisurely;
swallow'd This is a most pleasant and agreeable sto-
medicine which seldom fails

For Coughs & Consumptions

Drink freely of Colts foot Tea sweetned w.th Honey was
it is an excellent pectoral and a specific for all dise
of the Lungs (shred an handfull to a quart of boyling w
as Camomile is for intermittents Wild Carrot for the
and Tansey for the Gout they are all excellent in their

For Agues and Female Obstructio

pour a quart of Water on a pound or two of filings of
stir it about often pour of what swims and drink
of a pint daily add more Water as you need —
Remarks This is a preparation of Lemerys and better
than any one from Chymical proofs this is the best ph
Steel in being

192

To preserve Peaches in Brandy

To every twelve Peaches 3 quarters of a p of double
Refined Sugr and a gill of Spring water first
boyling the Sugr untill it is clear then take it
off the Fire and let stand till allmost cold ____
the Peaches must be ripe enough for eating
and must be rubed with a linnen cloath and
pricked full of holes wth a Needle when the Sugr
is almost cold put in the Peaches and set them
on a Slow Fire and let them Simmer a little ___
and with a bunch of Feathers keep the Peaches
under the Sugr as much as possible, then take
them out and put them into Jarrs and pour the
Syrup over them and lett them stand all Night
then take them out and give them a boyl untill
they are tender then put them into the Jarrs ___
and pour a little Brandy over them to harden them ___
then boil the Syrup a little skim it and let it stand
till cold and then put to every pint of Syrup half
a pint of Brandy then put it upon your Peaches
and cover them close wth Bladers and keep them
in a cool place

193

196

S.

for y Scotian-ague see Ague.
y Sicke. p. 37.
y Tooth-acke. p. 50. 56. 173.
roughness of y Toung: p. 114.
a Tympany. p. 52.
A Tysan. p. 166.

V.

to roste a legge of Veal. p. 137.
to bake Venison in a good crust. p. 137.
for y Biting of Venemous-beast. p. 98
to make Syrope of Viniger. p. 128.
for Vlcers. p. 115. 164.
Vnguentū aureū. p. 115.
an Vnguent for y Scabbe. p. 115.
for y Sores. p. 115.
Vnguents whote & colde. p. 97.
for Vometing. p. 39. 163.
to stay Vometing. p. 113.
to cleanse y Vrine. p. 40.
to make Vshebaugh. p. 155. 156. 157.
for y Vuula. p. 10. 23.

Vineg to make

W.

Washing-Balls. p. 29.
Waters cordiall. p. 97. 175
for Stephen's Water. p. 155.
(See Aqua.) Waters for Sore eyes. p. 170.
for a Webbe. see y eyes. for y eyes. p. 170.
a Wenne. p. 3.
to cure by y Weapon. p. 55.
for one y cannot make Water. p. 22. 23.
Rettime of Winde. p. 102. 57. 114. 117.
see Collicke.

w.

for Wormes. in y body. p. 114.
a plaister for Wormes. p. 56. 164. 165.
a Wound. p. 42. 43. 45. 47. 47. 48. 115. 115
a green Wound. p. 22. 39.
See to stay y Blood. Bruses. Iron. &c.
for y Wolf. p. 32.
for y fainting of Women. p. 162.
for Weaknass in Women. p. 165. 169.
see for y Back.
to Whiten fine yarn or cloath. p. 153.

Waters. to wash old Sores. p. 170.
for y Eyes. p. 170.

nephretick pills excelent for
y Stone ————— 179
to make Raspis berry an wine or
Gooseberry wine O ——— 180

Excell Plague or Surfeit water 181
To make Syrup of Clove July floars
182

An Excelent Eye water
for horse or man
or Good for chicken 183

the heele of Lard is —————
very good minced pyes 184/5
Excelent cure for an ague 184
To recover flatt drink y
it may be used on 3 dayes.
187

198

e r Balm Drops for a wound of any for
or any thing Comperable — — —
page 188
9

Composition for the Gout
190
Duffys Elixer
191
To make Shrub . . .
192
Excelent Shoe Blaiking See page 209) —
192
St Johns wort drops
}
reet for a Cold ·   } 193

Bramble Perry wine &cc. receipt for obte? of a mad dog
194
Cure the bite of a mad Dog . — 8 204 & 209
To Cure an Itch with Ease & Safty —— 207
Currant & Rasp Wine ye best way
203
For the Itch in human bodies or Mange in dogs see above
For a Cold when ill with a tickling Cough 208
Minced pyes, 209
pickle walnuts 210 and Receipe for the Jaundiees —
The Marquis of Granby receipe for Brewing 211
Cyder to Refine   211
Orange Ale ——— Do
Mrs Paxtons Eee for the Cholick 216
Andersons purging pills — 218
For a sprain of Musicsles by a stroke Fall or otherwise 220?
also Lady hodgsons Eye water —.———   }

199

To Boyl Yarn — very white ~~for 15 D~~ 20?
First boyl yr Yarn in yr Common way [th good ashes score]
wash [well] and dry it. Then take half pound
of pot ashes, half pd Sweet sope, 2 oz Roch
allum, 1 oz Spanish white, 2 oz stone
blew mix all togither and boyl your
yarn therein till it become white wch
it will be in about an hours time.
When you take it out of yr pot
or Kettle, have a Tub of Cold water
to put it into if instantly lest
yr heat tender it ~~unavoidably~~
deen where its carryd away to be ringed
before it ~~cools~~

Se July 20 6

To Every pound of yarn put 2 oz
and is ... by boyl'd without the common ashes
old coin clear by blew this is the best precept

tost

6 stowsares
8 toweles
4 fine hollin crostbothand i sengel cvostloth
i breth of skoth cloth for a rose edged
i breth of lavene edged
ii nett coues
iiii ✕ ✕ handkerchures
ii norve fallenge bandes of kambreke
ii pare of coufes norve

fyrst take a ... of an oz of gaules, beaten to ... pouder, an
... them ... a ... one ... of oyle of lin... one oz of
... of ... 3 or 4 ... on ... ... breaking
and ... ... them beate them to ... ... hand
full of ... ... a ... to ... of mutton ... ...
then beate them to ... ... them ... ...
... ... them ... ... it ... a ...
... or ... ... for ye emerodes.

Take one pottle of the ... ... and ... of ... ...
a handfull of ... a handfull of ... ...
... a handfull of ... a ... of a ... of
... in the ... and take ... ... a ...
of ... ... them, a ... full of ... and
... them ... a little ... tyme And boyle all ...
to ... ... untill they be boyled ... a q... ...
mornings and night take two or fower or half a dozen
... full and warme it ... drincke it ... ... it if
... think this will not ... the ... if it ... you,
... may ... ... more I dout not but this will
... for it hath ... ... hath had it this ... years.

A poulder for ye Eyees to be taken in drincke or pottage.
Take ... ... of sinamon, one peni ... of
Cloues, ... of the blessed ... being
dryed ... ... into pouder, at ... ... being
finely beat at the weight of them all, then ... at ... of
pouder of Eyebright at all the rest ... ways ... mingle all
to ... ... all ... when you will at you^r
pleasure, in pottage drincke or in ... ... especially
fayst in the morning at noone ... last at night

A preseruatiue against ye plague.
Take sage of ... Rue, Elderleaues, ... brambleleaues, of
... a handfull stampe them in a mortar altogether, ... strayne
them through a fyne linnen cloathe. A quart of white wyne, ... a
good quantitye of white wyne ... ... mingle them altogether,
put her to after of ... ouns of white ginger drinke this medicyn
one ... euery mornings for ... dayes together fasting
And you shall be ... for one hole yeare by ye grace of god.

And yf it fortune on ye ferbon ... yf ...
... of ye hand ... you take ... a powdero ... a spon
full of ... water, ... a spoonfull of water of ... and a
quantitye of ... put them togeder, ... you
drinke it, ... it shall put out the poison ... yf ... ye ...
appeare, you take ye leaues of elders, ... ls of ... brambles
and ... , stampe them togeder ... make a plaster therof,
and lay it to ye sore, ... it will ... out ye poison god willingo.

for an swellinge

take a quart of renit mylke, a pint ... full of ... , ...
... ... take ... you beat it in a morter to ...
take 4 hand full of ... ... your ... , ...
... of ... ...
And halfe a pound of ... a ... ... them
all to ... ...
... hand full of bartey meal, ... stir them all well to
... ...
... plaster will ... rose all ye ...
... ... god ... shall find ... ...
... ...

Angelica & Burritt, each a handfull,
Steny & Stranz ye Juce into possit=dronke
w the puder of 2 or 3 cloues, & a little
Nottmuga; drink it 2 or 3 days,

Of sacifrage roote and earbe ij handfull, of Philippendula
like quantetie of grunnnell seed j ounce, of ye kirnels of cherie
stones ij ounces, of aniesedes half an ounce, of leueres like
quontety, all thes dride and beaten to pouder finelie
searsed and taking so much as often as nedes as you can
ituke ypp with a franche crune and put into a reasonable
draught of parcely water distilled luke warme and
drinkin it fasting ij oures at ye least and waulkinge after
the taking therof

A note of Mrs
Barbara Lees Lessons on Virginalle
which the hath learned and can play them

j kaison		
jorkies	Pauane	Mr Jeroman
xvi	why aske yee	Docter Bull
	The Lo: Willoughbies Welcom home Mr Bird &c
dowkes	My trew Loue is to y grene wood gon Mr Fardinand
xviii	Loth to depart	Mr Ferdinand
	Pauan delight	Mr Bird.
heres iiii	The Marigold galiard	Mr Bird.
cokes ii	Fortune	Mr Bird
chekins	The Cradle Pauane	Mr Holborne
x	The first	
	The second	Courrantes Mr Bird.
giese	The third	
Jowes ii brawes		

ore
Inclita facundo concordat gratia vultu

Mr . Bird

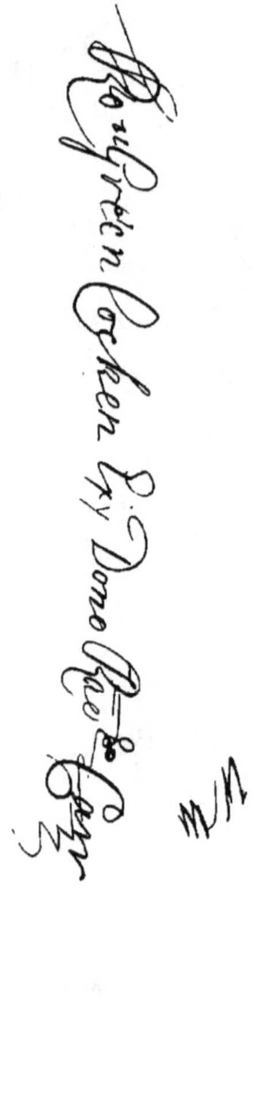